Savannah and Martin at 219 Harper's Cove

The Harper's Cove Series
Book 4

by
Deanndra Hall

Savannah and Martin at 219 Harper's Cove
The Harper's Cove Series Book 4

Celtic Muse Publishing
P.O. Box 3722
Paducah, KY 42002-3722

Copyright © 2014 Deanndra Hall
Print Edition
ISBN-13: 978-0692353691
ISBN-10: 0692353690

All rights reserved. Except as permitted under the U.S. Copyright Act of 1976, no part of this publication may be reproduced, distributed, or transmitted in any form or by any means, or stored in a database or retrieval system, without the prior written permission of the author.

This book is a work of fiction.

Names of characters, places, and events are the construction of the author, except those locations that are well-known and of general knowledge, and all are used fictitiously. Any resemblance to persons living or dead is coincidental, and great care was taken to design places, locations, or businesses that fit into the regional landscape without actual identification; as such, resemblance to actual places, locations, or businesses is coincidental. Any mention of a branded item, artistic work, or well-known business establishment, is used for authenticity in the work of fiction and was chosen by the author because of personal preference, its high quality, or the authenticity it lends to the work of fiction; the author has received no remuneration, either monetary or in-kind, for use of said product names, artistic work, or business establishments, and mention is not intended as advertising, nor does it constitute an endorsement. The author is solely responsible for content.

Cover design 2014 Celtic Muse Publishing, LLC, used by permission of the artist.
Formatting by BB eBooks

Disclaimer:

Material in this work of fiction is of a graphic sexual nature and is not intended for audiences under 18 years of age.

More titles from this author:

Love Under Construction Series

The Groundbreaking (Prequel)

The Groundbreaking is a preview of the main characters contained in all of the Love Under Construction Series books. Not intended as a work of erotic fiction, it is simply a way for the reader to get to know and love each character by discovering their backgrounds. Contains graphic situations that are unsuitable for readers under 18 years old.

Combo Volume: The Groundbreaking (Prequel) and Laying a Foundation (Book 1)

Sometimes death robs us of the life we thought we'd have; sometimes a relationship that just won't die can be almost as bad. And sometimes the universe aligns to take care of everything. When you've spent years alone, regardless the circumstances, getting back out there can be hard. But when you've finally opened up to love and it looks like you might lose it all, can love be enough to see you through?

Tearing Down Walls (Book 2)

Secrets – they can do more damage than the truth. Secrets have kept two people from realizing their full potential, but even worse, have kept them from forming lasting relationships and finding the love and acceptance they both desperately need. Can they finally let go of those secrets in time to find love – and maybe even to stay alive?

Renovating a Heart (Book 3)

Can a person's past really be so bad that they can never recover from it? Sometimes it seems that way. One man hides the truth of a horrific loss in his teen years; one woman hides the truth of a broken, scarred life that took a wrong turn in her teens. Can they be honest with each other, or even with themselves, about their feelings? And will they be able to go that distance before one of them is lost forever?

Planning an Addition (Book 4)

When you think you're set for life and that life gets yanked out from under you, starting over is hard. One woman who's starting over finds herself in love with two men who've started over too, and she's forced to choose. Or is she? And when one of them is threatened by their past, everyone has choices to make. Can they make the right ones in time to save a life?

The Harper's Cove Series

Karen and Brett at 326 Harper's Cove (Book 1)

Gloria wants more than anything to be invited to one of Karen and Brett Reynolds' parties, and she's very vocal about it. Karen and Brett, however, know full well that if Gloria were ever invited to one of their parties, she would be in a hurry to leave, and in an even bigger hurry to let everyone know they are the scourge of the neighborhood. Every Saturday night, Karen and Brett keep their secrets – all twelve of them.

Becca and Greg at 314 Harper's Cove (Book 2)

Even though they're quiet and stay to themselves, Becca and Greg Henderson seem pretty nice and average. They don't go out much or have many people over, except for that one couple who are probably relatives. But when that half-sister of Becca's moves in, it all seems a little fishy; she gets around pretty well for a person recovering from cancer. And where was Becca going all decked out in that weird outfit? The Henderson are tight-lipped, but Gloria hopes she can eventually get to the bottom of things. If she does, she'll get the biggest surprise of her life.

Donna and Connor at 228 Harper's Cove (Book 3)

Those nice people at 228, the Millicans? They're religious counselors, trying to help lovely couples who are having marital problems. Problem is, they're not counseling; training, maybe, but not counseling. But no matter what Donna says, Gloria still thinks the truck that delivered large crates to the Millicans' house in the wee hours of the morning, two weeks after they'd moved in, was pretty suspicious. Donna says it was exercise equipment that the moving company had lost, but Gloria's not so sure. Could it be that they're not as they appear?

Savannah and Martin at 219 Harper's Cove (Book 4)

Savannah and Martin McIntosh are new to the neighborhood, but that doesn't stop Gloria from trying her best to find out what they do on the second and fourth Friday nights of the month. Savannah insists they play cards, but Gloria's pretty sure it's more than that, considering the men she sees leaving the house in the wee hours of Saturday morning. But when she decides to get a little "up close and personal," she may get more than she bargained for.

The Me, You, and Us Series

Adventurous Me

Boring, tiresome, predictable ... all words Trish Stinson's soon-to-be ex-husband uses as excuses for why he's leaving after almost 30 years of marriage. But Trish's efforts to find adventure and prove him wrong land her in the lap of a man who leads her to an adventure she could've never predicted. And when that adventure throws her into a situation with a man who can't stand her, she's forced to decide between honor and her life.

Unforgettable You (Coming January 2015)

Reeling from a relationship that didn't happen, Steffen Cothran stumbles upon a woman who may be the answer to his prayers, but Sheila Brewster has problems he couldn't have anticipated. They work hard to forge a relationship, only to have it destroyed by someone from Steffen's past – the one person he'd forgotten about. As Sheila, hurt and angry, walks out of his life, Steffen eventually gives up on love until that fateful night when curiosity takes him somewhere he never thought he'd be to see something he never dreamed he'd see.

Incredible Us (Coming Fall 2015)

Dave Adams has just what he wants: Bliss, a well-respected BDSM club, all the subs a man could want, and a growing family who loves him. He expects his retirement years to be the best of his life – until he opens the club's back door and finds something, or someone, he could never have expected to find. He doesn't want to love Olivia Warren, over three decades his junior, but Dave is a natural protector, and he's never met anyone who needs protecting more than Olivia. Problem is, when her danger is over, he finds out that the relationship meant more than he ever dreamed.

The Celtic Fan (independent novel)

Journalist Steve Riley sets out to do the seemingly impossible: Find Nick Roberts, author of the bestselling book *The Celtic Fan*. When his traveling buddies lose interest, Steve continues on to a stolen address and finds someone who couldn't possibly be Roberts. As time goes by, Steve has to decide if he wants to break the story of a lifetime and break someone's heart, or give in to the feelings that promise him the love of a lifetime. Set in the beautiful Smoky Mountains of North Carolina, *The Celtic Fan* is both Steve's journey and excerpts from the original book written by Roberts about a young, wounded, WWII veteran and the forbidden love he finds.

A word from the author . . .

I never dreamed anyone would care much about these little novellas, but they're pretty popular! I love them because they're short, quick reads full of hot, crazy sex. This one is special in that I asked in a blog post for people to submit ideas for names for the characters. Every character in this book, with the exception of Gloria and Russell, was named by a fan. So let me give credit where credit is due.

- Tammy S. – Savannah and Martin
- Michele Mc – Harrison, Maura, and Ainsley
- Angel Blue – Tate
- Deborah B. – Marissa
- Charlene M. – Hayden
- Lora L. – Layla, Jeremy, Jasmine, and Tristan
- Felicity N. – Makayla
- Heidi – Stella
- Anna R. – Rowan, and Savannah and Martin's last name, McIntosh

Thanks to all of the readers who participated. I hope you'll enjoy reading about your characters in this book and keep reading the books to come. And thanks to my street team and support staff – you guys rock!

Love and happy reading,
Deanndra

Visit me at:
www.deanndrahall.com

Connect with me on my:
Substance B page

Contact me at:
DeanndraHall@gmail.com

Join me on on Facebook at:
facebook.com/deanndra.hall

Catch me on Twitter at:
twitter.com/DeanndraHall

Find me blogging at:
deanndrahall.blogspot.com

Write to me at:
P.O. Box 3722, Paducah, KY 42002-3722

Support your Indie authors!

Independent (Indie) authors are not a new phenomenon, but they are a hard-working one. As Indie authors, we write our books, have trouble finding anyone to beta read them for us, seldom have money to hire an editor, struggle with our cover art, find it nearly impossible to get a reviewer to even glance at our books, and do all of our own publicity, promotion, and marketing. This is not something that we do until we find someone to offer us a contract – this is a conscious decision we've made to do for ourselves that which we'd have to do regardless (especially promotion, which publishers rarely do anyway). We do it so big publishing doesn't take our money and give us nothing in return. We do it because we do not want to give up rights to something on which we've worked so hard. And we do it because we want to offer you a convenient, quality product for an excellent price.

Indie authors try to bring their readers something fresh, fun, and different. Please help your Indie authors:

- Buy our books! That makes it possible for us to continue to produce them;
- If you like them, please go back to the retailer

from which you bought them and review them for us. That helps us more than you could know;

- If you like them, please tell your friends, relatives, nail tech, lawn care guy, anyone you can find, about our books. Recommend them, please;
- If you're in a book circle, always contact an Indie author to see if you can get free or discounted books to use in your circle. Many would love to help you out;
- If you see our books being pirated, please let us know. We worked weekends, holidays, and through vacations (if we even get one) to put these books out, so please report it if you see them being stolen.

More than anything else, we hope you enjoy our books and, if you do, please contact us in whatever manner we've provided as it suits you. Visit our blogs and websites, friend our Facebook sites, and follow us on Twitter. We'd love to get to know you!

Savannah and Martin at 219 Harper's Cove

CHAPTER ONE

Savannah

I look around when I pull up in the drive. Nope – no nosy neighbor in sight. The car hasn't much more than stopped rolling when I jump out and run to the door before she can spot me and come charging over.

Gloria. The bane of my existence. We've only been in the neighborhood for about six months and already the woman is getting on my last nerve. Martin says to ignore her, but it's hard when she keeps coming around. I'd like to get to know more of the neighbors, but they're hard to meet. Apparently they all try to run from cars to houses to avoid her too. They wave, but I can't seem to catch them long enough to speak. Who can blame them? She's a real piece of work.

I clear the door easily. It isn't too hard, given that I've already clicked the security fob and the thing has swung open. It's a given that the system is unarmed too; I shut it off remotely before my car even rounded the corner. Once inside, I slam the door shut and take a deep breath before offloading everything I've brought in and dropping down onto the sofa in an exhausted heap.

Martin will be home in fifteen minutes so I need to start getting everything ready. I'll get a few things picked up, and I did the cleaning last night. There's not a lot left to do. All we need are the people.

CHAPTER TWO

Gloria

I've tried everything to get that weird McIntosh woman's attention, but she always runs to the house. I guess she needs to pee. I don't know why anyone would run that fast to get inside unless they were running from something.

I really believe there's something going on over there. Russell says to leave them alone, but you know, if they're doing something dangerous or weird, we all need to know, don't we? This is our neighborhood too, isn't it?

I'm still sure that picture with that horrible article in the paper was a picture of the Millicans. Russell doesn't think so; he says the woman's hair is too long. But I really think it's them. I can't believe that would be taking place right down the street, but I guess you never know.

Domination and submission. Sounds more like deprivation and subversion to me. Bunch of weirdos.

I'm got eyes on all of them. I'm pretty certain there are some weird things going on around this neighborhood. That pair, the Reynolds? I still don't know what was going on in their backyard that day. And what about the Hendersons? They had that woman living over there for awhile. Becca's sister, my foot. I still wonder what they were up to, especially after what I saw over there. Russell still doesn't believe me, but I know what I saw.

I asked Pete, the guy who owns the liquor store, what he thinks. His wife, Rosie, has been my friend for years, ever since they came to this side of town and opened their store. I go there for the gourmet foods. They have quite the variety. Pete says every neighborhood has one, a house where weird things go on, but now I'm pretty worried because this is way more than one. As far as I can tell, there's a whole bunch of oddballs around here. Russell and I are the only ones who seem even sort of normal.

Yeah, this neighborhood is going to the dogs, I tell you. No one else seems to care except me. I guess I'm all alone in this, so I'll do what I have to do.

Whatever that is.

CHAPTER THREE

Savannah

I put out the fishbowl. I've got prettier containers, but this one is kind of symbolic for us. It's been with us for a long time now, and I think if I changed it out, everyone would just ask where it was.

The food is almost ready, and everyone is bringing something, so it's not all on me. I get out the guidelines; I understand Rowan and Stella are bringing a new couple tonight. That gets my interest up. Stella said she's been trying to get them to come for some time and they've been reluctant, but she's finally talked them into it. I hope to god she's been very clear with them about what we do and how we do it. Anyone we bring in has to be approved beforehand and fully vetted.

Martin comes through the door all smiles and hugs. I know he hates that job; I hate that job *for* him. It's drudgery at its worst, but it pays the bills. If

I could get a teaching gig, that would at least give him time to go out and look for something a little better. But so far, no luck.

Layla and Jeremy are the first to show up. She fixed those little meatballs everyone loves so much – I could eat my weight in those. We talk about minor things, the car repairs I had to have done, the dog going to the vet, and then she asks me if there's any news about my nosy neighbor. I'm glad to report I haven't had a run-in with her in about two weeks. I'm pretty sure my luck's about to peter out.

They haven't been here for five minutes when Harrison and Maura show up. They're so much fun, and Harrison, well, he's a very talented guy. I've heard from Martin that Maura is pretty talented in her own right. They're followed by Marissa and Tate, then Makayla and Ainsley.

When Angel and Hayden get here, it's pretty clear something's been going on. I hate starting this any time one of the couples in the group has been having problems. If you didn't have them before, this will do it, so going in with a problem makes it problematic for everyone.

By the time Stella and Rowan show up, I'm getting kind of antsy. I'm wondering who this is they're introducing. They don't give us a hint, but she's all smug and winking.

Then the doorbell rings. When I answer it, I get

the biggest shock of my life.

What's standing on the other side of my door is a man over six feet tall with the most beautiful caramel-colored skin I've ever seen. If that wasn't enough, the dreadlocks he's wearing almost halfway down his back would've done me in. And those eyes – flecks of gold in a sea of chocolate. His lips are full and lush, his nose just wide enough for the rest of his face, and he's got almost sinister eyebrows, their cant enough to make a heart stop. He reminds me of Jason Momoa, only darker. He says in a breathy tone, "Are you Savannah?"

"Yes," I manage to squeak out. Damn. I'm going to embarrass myself, I can tell. Beside him is a woman who looks remarkably like . . . me.

"I'm Tristan. This is my wife, Jasmine. I was hoping this was the right place."

"Uh, yes, um, come in," I stammer. Everyone is staring when I look back at the room. "Everyone, this is Jasmine and Tristan." Martin takes over, thankfully, and finishes the introductions. I'm relieved. I can sit and stare. Most of the other women are staring too.

Dinner is casual. Somehow I can't help but keep staring at this new person and wondering what it would be like if I got his keys. I wish I could get a look at the fob, but he hasn't plopped them down in the bowl yet.

As soon as we've cleared the dishes, I start by saying, "Martin, why don't you remind everyone of the ground rules?"

He picks up the sheets of paper I pulled from the drawer, clears his throat, and stands. "First, the women choose. Always. And if you draw someone you don't want to go home with, then we put all of the keys back in the bowl and start all over. For example, if you drew the same person two weeks in a row, you might not want to follow through, which would be understandable." Everyone nods.

"Second, condoms. Always. No exceptions. I hope everyone brought a supply, and I believe every house in the group keeps plenty, am I correct?" Everyone nods.

"Third, everyone's out by six o'clock tomorrow morning. No exceptions. There will be no man in someone else's bed when he comes home. That's always been a rule, and that's not going to change. No threesomes; no foursomes. Couples only. We could get something started that we really don't want to continue in that fashion. Agreed?" Everyone nods. "Guys, we're all meeting at the Waffle Iron down the street for breakfast at six thirty, give the women time to clean up and get some rest while we compare notes. Everybody on?" All the guys nod in agreement.

"Fourth, you can't go home with your own man.

Against the rules. That kind of does away with the purpose of the group. So remember that. Okay then. I can't think of anything else. Anybody?" No one says anything, and several shake their heads. "Then welcome, Tristan and Jasmine. Are you ready to join this little group?"

"I just want to thank everyone for making us feel so welcome," Tristan says. I don't know if he's sincere or not. He's got to be uncomfortable with me staring at him the way I am, but I just can't help it. I haven't been able to take my eyes from him.

"You're quite welcome. So, ladies, make your choices." We all rise and go to the fishbowl.

It's been a custom of the men in the group to collect odd key fobs. We've had everything from troll dolls to rubber dinosaurs to bottle openers shaped like credit cards. They change them up every week, swap them around, get new ones to throw us, anything so none of the ladies know whose keys are whose. I'm glad of that or otherwise I would've made some choices over the years that were based on whose keys I could nab, and that wouldn't have been right. Along with the fun, this is an exercise in following through with choices and doing something we think we might not want to do. Cheating would've been counterproductive.

We draw numbers and Marissa goes first. She takes the keys with the weird little wrench key fob.

Then Makayla draws a set that I'm pretty sure are Martin's. I take the one with an odd symbol on it. I've never seen anything like it before, and I'd like to know more about it. You can bet I'll ask whomever they belong to.

So we go to our respective seats and Marissa holds up the keys she pulled. They're Jeremy's. Makayla's keys are Martin's – just as I thought. I could tell by his remote clicker. The pictures are worn off, and it's a Toyota, so that's pretty distinctive in this group.

Then I hold mine up. There's a pause, a long one, and a voice says, "Mine."

It's Tristan.

I can't believe it. That's not even possible. It's like my dreams and wishes drew him to me, and I had the good fortune of having Lady Luck actually hear them this time. As he looks at me, I wonder what he's thinking. And he smiles. That's a good sign.

We go on through the assignments. Everyone's happily paired, it seems. Jasmine draws Rowan, which is good; she takes home someone she already knows. This can be intimidating the first few times.

I don't have to go anywhere. One by one, the couples wander off, and pretty soon it's just me and Tristan. He turns to me.

"So what do we do from here? I've never done

this before."

"Well, first we sit down and kind of get to know each other. Do you want something to drink?"

"You having anything?"

"Hell yeah! I'm having a glass of wine."

His voice is dripping honey when he says, "I'll take whatever you're having." I draw out two stemless wine glasses and fill them full of a nice, warm pinot noir that I bought a couple of days earlier. We swirl the liquid and sit in silence for the first few sips.

Finally, Tristan breaks the silence. "So, have you ever been with a man of color before?"

I shake my head and my face turns red. "No, I have to admit I haven't. Not because I didn't want to. It just never happened." As I speak, I grab the bottom edge of my top and pull it over my head, then toss it to the floor.

He laughs. "Well, then let me assure you, the rumors are untrue. We're no different than any other man." He stops. "Any white man. It's just the brothers who are overly endowed who get the press. Not the rest of us." He's unbuttoning his shirt as he speaks and, when it's undone, he draws it off and tosses it onto the floor with my top. His chest is hard and smooth.

"That's a shame," I say without thinking, and he bursts into laughter. I like this guy. I mean, along with his looks, I really like him. He and Ainsley kept everyone laughing throughout dinner so he's got a good sense of humor, and I value that highly. "I'm sorry. That sounded kind of shallow, huh?" I chuckle. I'm undoing my jeans. Once they're unzipped, I shimmy out of them and they join the other clothes.

"No. That sounds honest, and I like that." He trails a fingertip up my arm. "We almost didn't come tonight."

"Oh? Why?" I imagine he's about to tell me that Jasmine didn't want to come, that she was afraid or something.

"I was afraid." I'm startled. This big, gorgeous, powerfully-built man was afraid? "I have problems opening up to people. I was abused as a child, and I really don't trust too many people. But you look pretty trustworthy, I guess," he says and smiles again.

"I try to be. What did Stella and Rowan tell you about the group?"

"They said you've been doing this for a good while. They said it was safe, consensual, and lots of fun. They said it would spice up our love life. It's pretty good already; if this pumps up the volume, I'm going to need more vitamins!" he laughs. He stands, unbuttons and unzips his slacks, and lets them fall, then steps out of them and sits back down. His black boxer briefs accentuate every ripple.

"It'll do it. We get together the second and fourth Friday nights of the month, and everyone looks forward to it. Think about it – it's like a mini vacation from life. Plus if someone doesn't show up, no big deal; we just have fewer keys to choose from, that's all." He reaches over and unhooks my bra for me, and I draw it off and throw it in the pile.

His visual assessment of my breasts makes me suck in a breath, and he nods. "Makes sense. Have you ever been to an orgy?"

I shake my head. "Nope. I'd like to sometime, though. But it would have to be a group of people I really trusted, and I don't know that many."

"This is damn near a big enough group already, don't you think?" he asks, and continues to stroke my arm. Then he moves a little closer to me.

"Very nearly." I turn my face to his and he draws it to him and kisses me.

Warm and soft. His lips are amazing. He nibbles my lower lip and I nearly come undone. His hands wrap around my waist and one travels up my back, up my neck, and wraps itself into my hair tight. Then he yanks my hair and pulls my head back to kiss my neck.

I almost come from the sheer intensity of his touch. It's like sparks radiating out all over my skin. My blood shoots to boiling and warms everything inside me, and I go wet – soaking wet. I want this man. I'm not sure why he has the effect on me that he has, but I want him like I've never wanted another man in this group. We've got a good-looking bunch, and it's been hard over the years to remember that we're not supposed to be emotionally attached, but this is something else entirely. It's like a drug coursing through my veins for the first time, and I'm almost overwhelmed by the sensation.

"Let's take this upstairs, shall we?" he asks, and I'm happier to hear those words than I have been any others in a long, long time. I nod. "Here." He stands, takes my glass, places it on the table for me, and draws me up against him. Can he feel my hard nipples against his chest? I'm guessing so, because a hand comes around and cradles one of my breasts while the other travels down to my ass and cups one cheek. I'm in heaven, and I still have my panties on.

"Bedroom?" he says, pointing up the stairs. I nod, mute. "Let's go." He sounds more like a ten-year-old boy going to his first swim meet than a man going upstairs with a woman he doesn't know to have sex. And I feel like a thirteen-year-old girl going to her first boy/girl party. It's crazy, I know, but this guy does something to me.

The bedroom door is open, but he closes it behind us, then grabs my arm and slams me up against it. I feel the panels in the door cutting into my shoulders. Both of his hands are on my face, and he kisses me, another long, hot kiss that makes me pant when he turns loose. He takes my hand and leads me to the bed, turns me around, and presses me down to sit. I'm almost at the perfect level to suck him, but that's not what he's got in mind.

Top edge of my panties in his fingers, he kneels in front of me and begins to pull them downward, so I rise up just a smidge to allow them to come down. When he's got them down to my ankles, I pick up my feet and he whisks them off, then tosses them toward the door. A big, firm hand rests on each of my knees, and he presses my legs apart.

"Ah. Beautiful. You smell lovely. May I?" he asks, nodding toward the apex of my thighs.

I can barely speak. "Please. Take charge."

There's a flicker of something across his face. He makes his way between my thighs and licks the inside of each one, sending shivers up my spine that I can't control. My hard nipples turn to stainless steel, so hard they burn. That tongue explores my mons, my lips, and then finds its way into the entrance of my pussy. It's hot and strong, and I feel it curl as it travels up between my labial lips and finds my pearl, just at the top of the divide. The curling goes around its perimeter and then straight up its center, and I arch my back and fall backward, landing on my elbows.

"I'm not going to make you come this way," he whispers to me. "I just want to watch you squirm."

Squirm. I'm uncomfortable with squirming. I need more than to just squirm, but he sets about torturing me. If this is what his wife gets every night, she's one lucky, lucky, very lucky woman. It's unbearable heaven and I'm beyond turned on. Digging my fingers into his scalp as he laps at me, I run my hands down his dreads, and I hear him moan, a deep, throaty sound that makes me even needier than I already was. When I'm right at the edge, he stops, then presses two fingers into my cunt.

I almost scream. The pressure is disarming, and then he begins to pump. I'm slapping my toes on the floor, begging without words, and he knows it. Just when I think I can't take another second, he stops, climbs up onto the bed, and pulls me up from the edge and into the center, my head on the pillows. "Savannah, I want to fuck you so bad. Are you ready?"

"Ohhhhh, god, yes. I want it too." I can barely speak. Those firm, hot lips cover mine and I'm floating away on a river of passion, something so deep and dark that it doesn't have words. His tongue rakes along mine, a scalding rubbing, and I moan into his mouth. I feel him reposition himself as he kisses me and, before I know it, my legs are forced apart by his knees and he's kneeling between them. As he's kneeling, he's taking off his briefs, and when he finally breaks the kiss and rises to his knees between my legs, I almost faint.

His cock is amazing. It's got a huge, throbbing head, and his shaft is almost as big around as my wrist. I'm staring – I can't help it. It's just so, well, I've never seen anything like that in my *life*. I want to reach out and grab it, but all I can manage to squeak out is, "May I suck you?"

"Nope." He smiles, then rolls on a condom. "I want to fuck you, Savannah. I want to be all the way up in that pretty little pink pussy of yours, burning up all those juices you've worked up with the friction I'm going to pour on. Are you ready for that? Do you want me to fill you up, sweetness?"

"Oh, hell yes. Please, please, fill me up." I'm barely able to breathe. I want this and I want it right now.

He slips his hands into the hollows behind my knees, lifts me up so my ass is on his thighs, and positions the head of his cock in the entrance to my pussy. I really am squirming now; I don't want to wait anymore. Then he grins at me, a pretend-evil grin that makes me smile. "Beg me. I want you to be my whore. Beg me for my dick. I'll ram you if you'll beg like a slutty girl."

"Please, oh god, please fuck me!" I'm frantic

now. "Please, Tristan, please? I need it so bad. Please, please, pretty please?"

"That's pretty good begging! I'm impressed. Now say, 'Shove your cock into my pussy, stud.' I want to hear you say it."

"Shove your cock into my pussy, stud. Please? Hard?"

When the word "hard" comes out of my mouth, he pulls back slightly and rams me with all his might. I almost come up off the bed. The shriek that comes from between my lips shocks even me. With that, he starts an almighty pumping that would put most men to shame; well, most of the men *I* know. He's powering into me full-throttle, and the stretch he's giving my sheath is epic. On top of that, the angle he's using is scrubbing across my g-spot, and my orgasm is gaining ground with every thrust. It's almost intolerable. I don't know what to do to make it stop, or make it go faster, or make it . . . at this point, I'm not sure what I want.

Looking up, his tempered chest and biceps make me swoon. They're some kind of glorious. *He's* some kind of glorious. None of the other guys in our group are built as powerfully as this, all muscle and brawn. His skin is glossy with sweat, the sheen on its darkness making his muscle definition even clearer.

But it's the way he looks down at me, like he's going to eat me alive, devour me, suck me into him and never even spit out a bone, that makes the want inside me grow and spiral and twist, and I'm finding it hard to breathe. I let out a hoarse, "I'm gonna come. Come with me, Tristan, please?"

"Go ahead and come, baby. Ride the crest of the wave." Instead of just stroking into me, now he's stroking and, at the same time, using his hands under my knees to push me out and pull me back into him in rhythm with his stroking. His cock head is hitting bottom over and over, making me almost squeal, and I feel the clenching of every muscle in my abdomen before, without warning, I shriek out, "Oh my god! I'm coming!" and I turn loose.

My hips are bucking out of control and my hands are gripping my breasts, squeezing them, pulling my nipples and twisting them, and he's still going, still pounding into me. "Oh god," I groan out in an unfamiliar, strained voice I don't ever remember hearing coming from my mouth before. And just when I think I can't take another second, I feel him slam into me, then grind, and grunt a few times as he fills his condom.

But instead of falling onto me, he runs his hands down my legs, grips my ankles, and holds them behind his ass as he leans back on them. I watch him as he stares down his chest and belly straight into the spot where his shaft disappears into my wetness. "Sweet lord, my prick looks good buried in your pretty pussy, girlie," he grins.

I need to start again – immediately. "Oh, god, I need you to fuck me again, Tristan, please?"

He laughs, then drops down over me onto his hands, staring down into my face. "How was that?"

I drag my hands through my hair absentmindedly. "Amazing. Incredible. I want more."

"Ah, it's time for that sucking you wanted to give me. Do you still want to suck me?"

"Oh, hell yes! Here, I'll do that," I say as he leans back again, and I roll the condom off his cock and throw it in the trash. He's still on his knees on the bed, leaning back with his hands, his back arched toward me, and I drop to my elbows and take his softness into my mouth.

He goes hard instantly. It's like I can *feel* it growing on my tongue. Before more than a few seconds have gone by, he's rock-hard and I'm struggling to get him all the way into my mouth. I take the head of his cock down my throat and he lets loose with a roar. "Oh, yeah, suck me! Take it all, cock-sucking little bitch. I love your tongue. Suck me good!" No one's ever talked to me like that, and it takes the fire already between my legs to inferno proportions. I just want to taste his cum down my throat like a flood, and he's well on his way. I'm not surprised when he says, "I'm taking over, baby. Here we go." He threads his big hands into my hair and drags my face down over him.

His cock goes down my throat – hard. I gag but he drags me onto him again, and I finally find a way to open up enough to let the head down into my throat. He's slamming deep into my velvety pinkness, and I'm trying to stay open so I don't choke. "Oh yeah, that's so good, so good. You're good at the deep throat thing, really, really good. I'm gonna give you all the spunk you can handle, slut, yes I am." He sucks breath in between his teeth and I'm going insane, my hands on his thighs, wishing I could stroke my clit while I'm sucking him.

I try to push back a little, but Tristan barks, "Hands out! Arms straight out! I'm in charge, girl. I'll fuck your face the way I like. Arms out!" he yells again, and I force my arms straight out perpendicular to my body. He's dragging my face up and down on his shaft. I'm no longer in control in any way, and I'm so turned on I feel like I'll faint. He starts to growl, "Ohhh, ohhh, I'm gonna come, I'm gonna come, slut. You'll swallow it, slut, every drop, you hear me? Swallow my cum, girl. Ohhh, ohhh god, here it comes. Here it comes. Get ready to swallow. Get ready. Ahhhhhhh . . ." I feel the flood, the heat, taste the salty bitterness, and it's everywhere, down my throat, bubbling out around my lips, under my tongue, pooling in my cheeks. "Awwww, yeah, swallow me down," he snarls again, and I'm swallowing as fast and deep as I can.

Once I've gotten it all down, I start to lick him clean. To my surprise, he lets out something that sounds like a whimper, then falls onto the mattress. Before I can get it all licked up, he grabs my arm and pulls me up to him, rolling on top of me, kissing me hard and deep. My whole body is on fire when I say, "Can you taste yourself on me? Taste your cum in my mouth?"

He kisses me twice more. "Yeah, I do. God, you're something else. I hope you didn't mind me talking to you like that, but it really turns me on."

"Turns me on too," I grin. "Nobody's ever talked to me like that before. I like it."

"Does anybody else fuck your face like that?" he asks with a lopsided grin.

"Nope. And I love that too," I grin back.

"Good! We're on the same wavelength. That makes everything better." He kisses me again and I'm awash in sensation. "Get up on your hands and knees. I want to fuck your ass."

He doesn't have to tell me twice. He lubes me up, lubes up his wrapped rod, and then bores into me. While he pumps into my ass, he reaches around me and strokes my clit. I wouldn't even say he's pumping into me; it's more like a dog hunching another dog. It's raw and unsettling in a very hot way. I come violently. Once I'm done, he grabs a handful of my hair, yanks my head back, and fucks into me like there's no tomorrow, my asshole burning with the stretch. When he's filled that condom, he drops onto the mattress and pulls me into his side.

"Wondering how Jasmine's doing?" I ask when we're both still.

"Yeah. I've never shared her with anybody before." He stops for a second, deep in thought, then says, "She's never shared me with anybody else either. Wonder how she's feeling about that?"

I trace around one of his dark nipples. "The first time we did it, it was kind of a shock. After that, though, it was okay. I look forward to it now. All of the guys in the group are very sexually talented, so I'm always satisfied. I like them all; I can't say there's any one that I like better than all the rest. They're all so different, but they're all so good. Being with women other than their wives makes them stay on their toes, learn new sexual material, try new things. Then we're treated to the results of their adventures in our own bedrooms. It's great. Martin and I have really grown sexually as a couple since we've been swinging."

Tristan has a thoughtful look on his face. "I see what you're saying. So let me ask you something: Has Martin come home telling you that one of the other women has done something for him that you'd balked at before?"

I nod slowly, a little embarrassed. "Yeah. He came home one night and told me that Layla let him fist her. I hadn't ever let him do that to me."

"And?" Tristan grins at me in curiosity.

"I let him fist me the very next evening. I didn't want him to go back to her for something I wouldn't do for him, and I found out that's he's really good at it and I like it. I've had to be willing to deliver whatever everyone else is delivering or risk feeling inadequate. It's really made me grow as a sex partner."

"That's interesting." Tristan's fingers have found my nipple and they're pinching and tweaking it over and over. "Wonder what Jasmine's experience will be?"

We fucked all night long – and I mean all night long. At five thirty on Saturday morning, he leads me down the stairs with his boxer briefs in his hand. Once we're downstairs, he puts on his shirt, then bends me over the arm of the sofa and fucks me one last time. When he finishes, he throws away his condom, draws on the rest of his clothes, then kisses me, smacks my ass with his hand, and grins when he says, "Keep it real, pretty pussy." He blows me a kiss as he closes the door behind him.

I smile as I wonder what they'll be talking about down at the Waffle Iron. Do they talk about us? Martin has assured me that they do. There are no secrets. Might as well not be – every one of them will be sleeping with every one of us eventually. But I'd still love to hear that conversation.

CHAPTER FOUR

Gloria

When I go out to pick up the newspaper from the driveway, I see a strange sight. There's a black man leaving the McIntoshs' house. I look at my watch. It's ten after six in the morning. And I don't see Mr. McIntosh's car in the driveway. Wonder what that's about.

"Russell, there's a colored man leaving the McIntosh's house. And Mr. McIntosh's car isn't there."

He doesn't even look up from his pancakes. "So?"

"So, don't you think that's weird?" Even Russell has to agree that it's strange.

"It's none of my business." He keeps shoveling pancakes into his piehole. "And that's politically incorrect. It's black, not that other word."

"Really, Russell, that's all you're concerned with? If the neighborhood's going down the toilet, it's everybody's business." I get tired of him saying that to me. I mean, if there's something going on over there, we all should know.

"Gloria, I've told you a million times and I'll tell you again: Stay out of the neighbors' business. I mean it."

I keep watching. At about twenty after seven, Mr. McIntosh's car comes pulling up into the driveway. I'd like to run out and try to catch him, talk to him for a minute, but it's kind of early and he'd probably wonder why I was out at that time of the morning.

But I can tell you this: I'll be watching that house for awhile, oh yes I will. I'm already sure there's some perverted stuff going on at some of the other neighbors' houses. If there's something going on over at the McIntoshs' house, I'm going to find that out too.

Wonder what Mr. McIntosh would say if I told him what I saw?

CHAPTER FIVE

Savannah

On Tuesday I almost make it into the house when I hear someone crying out, "Mrs. McIntosh! Mrs. McIntosh!"

Damn. It's her.

"Hi, Gloria. What can I do for you?" I've got my keys in my hand and I'm still edging toward the house.

"Hi!" She's out of breath from running toward me. "I just wanted to check and see if you were all right."

"I'm fine. Just fine. Why would you ask?" What is she up to?

She's still gasping. "I just wanted to make sure. I saw that big black man coming out of your house last Saturday morning."

Shit.

Now what? She's watching our house. What does she think we're doing every other Friday night?

Before I can finish the thought, she says, "So what exactly is going on over here on those Friday nights?"

Damn. *Think, Savannah.* "We play cards. Every other Friday night. It's a big thing for us."

"Really? Oh, that sounds like fun!" *Uh-oh*, my brain screams, and it's not for no reason. "I'd love to come sometime and play, Russell and I, I mean."

"Well, actually, we've been doing this for some time now. We're really, really close friends, and . . ."

"You can never have too many friends, now can you?" she twitters nervously.

Yes, you can, if one of them is you, I think to myself. "It's a closed group. The others like it that way, and I'm not one to ask them to change their minds."

She seems sad but satisfied with that answer. "Well, if you ever change your minds, let me know. We'd love to come over sometime." Before I can get away, she asks the twenty million dollar question: "So why was that guy leaving so early in the morning? And where was Mr. McIntosh?"

I've already spun toward the door and I'm running. "I've really got to get moving, Gloria. Everyone will be here pretty soon. Nice talking to you." I make it through the door and shut it behind me, then lean against it. Oh, goddamn. She's been watching our house. I'm surprised she hasn't noticed the guys leaving before, and then I realize – maybe she has. Maybe she's seen every one of them.

I'll be glad when Martin gets home. I don't know what to do. What can we do?

I've got everything ready when he walks through the door. "We need to talk," I tell him, and he can see from the look on my face that it's serious.

"What's wrong? You look like you've seen a ghost." He strokes my cheek and I almost cry as I recount the conversation I'd had with Gloria. "Oh, shit," he whispers. "I don't know what to do. What do we do?"

"I think . . ." and then a thought hits me. "I think from now on me and whomever I draw should just go to a hotel. I'll stay there when he leaves, and you can come and pick me up at the hotel and bring me back home with you. It's not a very good solution, but for now it's all I can think of."

"Unless," he says, "unless you want to just go ahead and do what we've been doing. So what if she finds out? What's she going to do?"

"She could make it very, very hard for us here in the neighborhood." I'm scared to death they'll push us out.

"How so?"

"How do you think the neighbors would feel about us?" I'm trembling.

Martin laughs. "How do they feel about *her*? That's the question you should be asking. And the answer is, they don't like her any more than we do. I think they'd toss *her* out if they could. And I can't believe we're the only ones on this street having any fun. Someone else has to be doing something that would look questionable."

Hmmmm . . . maybe he's right. Maybe someone else is doing something that she wouldn't like. Maybe they all would turn against her and back us. Before I can say anything, he asks, "Are you ready to scrap our lifestyle because of her?"

"Hell no," I blurt out. I'm not. To hell with Gloria Livingston. I'll fuck whomever I please.

I know I can't be with Tristan two weeks in a row; that's a rule. But I really, really want to. I'm insanely jealous when he winds up with Angel. And I wind up with Hayden. When they came through the door, it was obvious once again that something's going on between the two of them. This week, Martin goes with Jasmine, and I have to wonder how that will go.

Once everyone else is gone, Hayden is still sitting on the sofa. I can't help it; I just feel compelled to ask him what's wrong. "Do you want to talk for awhile?"

"About what?"

"About what's going on with you and Angel. Everyone sees it. You might as well come clean, honey."

He sighs. "Is it that obvious?" I nod. "Things just aren't going very well."

"Meaning?"

He shakes his head. "You won't like it."

That alarms me a little. "What do you mean, I won't like it?"

He looks up at me and locks eyes with me. "She wants to leave me for one of the men in this group." I wait, afraid of what he's about to say. "Savannah, it's Martin."

My heart nearly stops. "Martin?"

He nods. "Yep. She says she's in love with him."

I rake through my memory, but I can honestly say I haven't had any clue that Martin might feel the same way. Before I get a chance to say anything else, Hayden says, "Of course, two months ago it was Rowan. And three months before that, it was Jeremy." I start to relax a little. "We started doing this because she wanted to. And now I see why. I don't think it's them. I think it's anyone but me."

I feel sorry for the guy. He's trying to please his wife, and this is what happens. I take his hand. "Let's go upstairs and lose ourselves for the night, whaddya say? Forget about all of that. And tomorrow I'll have a talk with Martin about this, see if we can come up with something that will help you – help you both."

"Maybe you shouldn't . . ."

"Yes. I should. And now we should. Come on." I stand and reach for his hand. "Let's go. Let's make the most of the night. It's not like we've never spent the evening together before and, as I recall, it's always been fun. So let's do it again!" I wink at him and he finally smiles, then stands and takes my hand, and we head up the stairs.

"You know, I think I'd like to shower," Hayden says when we get upstairs. "Want to join me?"

My eyebrows lift and I shrug. "Sure! That sounds pretty good. Toothbrushes are . . . well, you know where they are." I start the water and step into the steamy embrace of the rainfall effect. Within a minute, Hayden is right there, and his arms wrap around my waist. His hands travel like satin up my ribcage and cup my breasts, and strong fingers and thumbs twist and pull my already-hardened nipples. I can't help but moan.

"You know, Savannah, of all the women in this group, you're the one I'm most comfortable with. You're just open and honest, and you're easy to talk to." He kisses the side of my neck. "I've always had a good time with you. And your pussy . . ." He bends me forward until my arms are folded onto the built-in bench in the shower and I feel him move into place behind me. "Oh, god, I need to be buried inside you. I hope you're ready."

I'm not, but I know he needs this, needs to feel like a man, like someone wants him. "I need it too, Hayden. Just take me, please?"

He presses his hardness into my softness, and I let out a low moan when he slides into my depths. I was readier than I thought, and I have no trouble taking him. He strokes in a consistent, pleasant rhythm, and it lights me up like a Christmas tree. The longer he strokes, the tighter and hotter I get, and I find myself squirming and pressing back against him. I love the feel of his fingers as they dig into my waist, pulling me back against him as he moves forward. He groans out, "Oh, Savannah, you feel so good, baby. I need to unload right now. Please? Can I do that, please?"

Suddenly I'm sorry for him, sorry for what Angel's putting him through, sorry that he feels like he has to beg a woman to get what he wants. "Do it, sweetie. Just do it. I'm right here with you." There's that sudden lengthening and thickening, and then there's a warmth in the condom that I can actually feel. When he's spent, he leans down over my back and wraps his arms around me. That's when I feel it – he starts to tremble.

I'm pretty sure he's crying, and I don't quite know what to do. "Hey, honey, let's get out and get dried off, okay? I'm turning into a prune!" I try to make light of everything, and we get out and towel off.

Before I can finish, he says, "Let me. Please? I want to." He takes the towel out of my hands and, before I can protest, he starts to towel me off. It's a gentle, caring kind of thing, and I'm suddenly caught off guard by this man's tenderness and consideration. There's no lecherousness here, just a good, solid man trying to be a gentleman. I've always liked Hayden, but now I really respect him too.

When he's finished drying me off, I smile at him and I think of something. "Thanks, Hayden. Hey, come on! I want to do something for you!" I lead him into the bedroom and point to the bed. "Stretch out on the bed and get comfortable. Face down." When he's all laid out, I climb up and straddle his legs. Starting with his shoulders, I massage deep and hard. A deep groan leaves his throat and I can feel him relaxing under my hands, the tightened muscles giving way and smoothing out. My hands work out the knots I find and then move downward until I'm working the tightness out of his waist, manipulating everything on either side of his spine as I go. When my hands finally make it to the small of his back, he turns his head enough to be able to see me out the corner of his eye.

"Savannah, that feels so good." He takes one of my hands, draws me off him, and then rolls over. His cock is hard and throbbing, and I feel every muscle between my legs draw up and tense in anticipation. Hayden rises up on his knees, wraps his big hands around the back of my neck, and kisses me. "Do you want me, little one? Do you want me to fill you up over and over?" he moans into my mouth.

I whisper back to him, "Yes. Make me scream, babe. Make me come."

Quick as a wink, he's got me down on the mattress, and he slides down between my legs and plants his face in my sex. His tongue is sandpaper on my swollen bud, and I writhe and moan, my fingers tangled in his hair, holding him down, begging with my hips for him to keep going. He's talented at what he's doing, and in minutes I come with a cry, my hips churning and shaking.

When he finally stops, he looks up at me and grins. "Good?"

I grin back at him. "Good? No. Great! Get up here and fill me up, stud." In a flash he's beside me, his arms around my waist, pulling me into him. One glance at his face and I see something I haven't seen before: Gratitude. That was completely unexpected, and it takes me completely by surprise. I stroke the side of his face and watch his expression change, from lust to something softer and sweeter.

"You're really enjoying this, aren't you?" he whispers.

I nod and smile. "Yes. I really am. You're great in the sack, Hayden. No complaints here."

He kisses me. It's not the usual expected or required kiss. It's genuine, something between a thanks and an invitation to pour myself into him. It's . . . nice. Very nice. Comfortable even. And in that moment I realize that I really *am* enjoying myself. I also realize that I haven't thought about Tristan all night, and I haven't thought about Martin since we talked about Angel earlier. It's refreshing, actually, to be that removed from the things that take up my everyday thoughts and to be put in a position where I'm just thinking about myself and the man I'm with and what's happening in that moment. I kiss him back and feel that connection, almost familial, but with a hint of raw sexuality. He presses the head of his cock into my folds and I tip my pelvis to meet it, and in a second he's slipped inside me and pumping.

And I'm carried away. I slip toward ecstasy with Hayden as my guide, and his hands and mouth guide me along the way, making it easier for me to go there than it has been in a long, long time. Does Angel appreciate this, the vulnerability and willingness to bare his feelings, that I'm experiencing with her husband? Is he this transparent with her? If he's not, he should be. I have to ask: "Do you and Angel make love this way?"

He shakes his head and a sad look comes over his face. "No. She wants all kinds of acrobatics and performance art. I just want to love her, but she's not interested in that." And that's a shame, because the need is rolling off this man, the desire to have someone tell him that he's good and kind and decent. I run my hands up his back, up into his hair, and he leans down, kisses me, and moans into my mouth. I feel him relax first and then begin to tense as he gets closer to the ultimate goal. All of the heat and craziness is rising in me too, my breathing quickening and my heart rate soaring.

Hayden groans, "Oh, yeah. Oh, Savannah, baby, come with me?"

I nod fast and hard. "I want to, Hayden. I really do. Faster, please?" He gives it all he has, and I'm right there. Then I tip over the edge, my tightness gripping him even tighter, and he grunts and slams into me repeatedly, then falls on top of me.

When he's had a chance to catch his breath, he surprises me by rising up on his hands, leaning down, and kissing me. When he pulls back, he simply says, "Thanks, Savannah. Thanks for being nice to me."

"You're easy to be nice to! You're a good guy, Hayden. Don't let anyone tell you otherwise." He drops down onto the bed beside me and stares at the ceiling. "Penny for your thoughts."

He sighs. "I'm just thinking about how I really don't want to go home."

My heart breaks for him. "Hey, don't think about it. We've got hours left. Let's just have some fun! Let's go play in the living room. Or the kitchen." I take his hand and pull him up from the bed and toward the hallway.

"Or right here," he growls, then grabs my arm and spins me around, trapping me between his body and the wall. "I want you again, Savannah. Right now." I can feel his cock straining against my belly and, quick as a wink, he lifts me up with his hands under my thighs and drops me down, impaling my pussy on his hardness. A shriek pops out of my mouth and he starts to pound into me, a relentless driving that surprises and thrills me. It's delicious, so fast and hot. I wrap my arms around his neck and hang on, and when I bite his earlobe, it's game on.

He's slamming me against the wall with his thrusts, fast and furious, the scent of our sex filling the space right around us, and everything inside me starts to melt. He's turned into the epitome of maleness, uncaring when it comes to my satisfaction, just using my body as his release, his plane of pleasure, and my arousal hits an all-time high for the night. It's as heady and thrilling as anything I've done in weeks, even with Tristan. "Do you like it, baby? Tell me if you like it."

"I don't like it. I love it. Damn, fuck me, Hayden. Just keep fucking me," I manage to pant out. In under two minutes I'm shaking with my climax, and Hayden keeps going, his shaft piercing me over and over, a staccato tempo like a string of firecrackers going off. "Keep going, baby, don't stop."

The tension in his shoulders and neck is bound to be unbearable, and then he whispers, "You fuck so damn good. I can't stop." I'm beginning to believe that it's true – it's going to go on forever, and right at the moment that's fine with me. A couple of minutes later I hear him mutter, "Shit, I'm gonna come. Oh, god, Savannah, I'm gonna come." He keeps going and finally yells out, "Oh yeah! Oh my god, baby, oh my god!"

Hayden rests against me, his forehead pressed against mine, still holding me up and on his cock. I'm sure he's exhausted until he says, "Want to get back in the shower?"

"Sure! I'd love it!" I've always loved showering with a man. It just seems more primitive to me than any other setting. And it's not something Martin is crazy about, so this is a good opportunity for me to get my mojo on.

While the water heats up, I light some candles and turn out the ceiling lights. Hayden is behind me, stroking my back the whole time, and when I finally turn around he plants a hot, firm kiss on my neck, nibbling afterward, and I melt. I reach down and find his cock, firm and waiting, and lead him by it into the shower. Once in, I kneel in front of him and take him in my mouth, all of him, slowly and down my throat. The moan that escapes his lips makes my whole body hum with anticipation. I start to stroke down onto him, tasting his pre-cum, that sour, salty taste I love, and I moan around his shaft.

Before the vibration from my moan can die, his hands wrap in my hair and pull me down over him, and he begins a purposeful thrusting into my throat. I feel myself growing wet again, and I can feel my clit pulsing and swelling. In minutes he cries out and fills my mouth and throat, his bitter creaminess warming me. As soon as his cock stops twitching, Hayden pulls me to my feet.

His arms wrap around my waist and he kisses me. This isn't your garden variety kiss, no. It's as steamy as the water pounding down on us from the showerhead, and it goes on for what seems like forever. When it ends, I open my eyes to find Hayden's searching my face. In a near whisper, he says, "Savannah, can I ask you something? Will you be honest with me?"

I nod. "Of course."

His face reddens, then he manages to stammer out, "If Angel leaves me, do you think any other woman would want me?"

I fight the urge to laugh, but I can't hide my smile. "Are you kidding? They'll be fighting over you!"

"No, really, don't try to make me feel good, just tell me the truth. I can take it."

At that, I shake my head and the laughter just pops out. "I'm not lying to you. They'll be fighting over you, I promise. You're a great guy, a decent and smart guy, and you're good-looking too. And you're polite and considerate. Not to mention that you're a helluva lover. You won't have any trouble if it comes to that. But I hope it doesn't come to that."

A thoughtful look spreads across his face. "You know, maybe it should. Maybe I've been hanging on too long. Maybe I should just let her go. I mean, it's obvious that she's unhappy, and I love her but she's making *me* unhappy. Maybe I should just let go and let her go out to find the happiness she wants. Then I could maybe find some too." It's like he's had an epiphany and suddenly I'm proud of him.

"Well, I can tell you this, she'll be hard pressed to ever find another guy as good as you. I don't want to see you two break up, but I would like to see both of you happy, especially you. You deserve it." With that, I give him a huge, genuine smile.

He grins back. "Thanks. I appreciate that. You're a good person, Savannah. If we break up and I have to leave the group, I'm just glad I got to know you,

you and Martin both. You're good people."

I take him by the hand and lead him out of the shower, then take a few minutes to carefully and gently dry him. When he's done the same for me, I hand him a robe, take mine, and say, "Let's take a break. Let's go downstairs, fix some coffee, have a brownie or something and just talk."

He gives me a small, sad smile. "I'd like that a lot."

"Have a good time last night?" Martin asks as he comes through the front door. He drops his jacket on the sofa and makes his way to me, his arms wrapping around my waist. His lips are on mine in a second, and he kisses me long and deep before I pull back.

"We need to talk." I take his hand and pull him to the sofa.

He cuts his eyes toward me and watches me from the corners of them. "What did I do wrong?"

"Nothing, babe! But there's something I think you need to know." I spend the next thirty minutes telling him all the things Hayden said. I watch his face go from sadness to alarm to confusion.

"What do we do?"

I shake my head. "Nothing we can do. They have to figure this out for themselves."

Martin grins at me and presses me down onto the sofa, climbing on top of me and kissing my neck and ear. I giggle. Then I call out, "Wait! Wait! How did it go with Jasmine?"

He sits up and sighs. "Oh my god, the woman is a crazy fuck."

"As in crazy good?" I'm sitting now, staring at him.

"As in crazy great. I felt like I was with a call girl. I don't think there's anything the woman wouldn't do. First thing she asked was if I wanted to tie her up and spank her. If that wasn't enough to turn me on, you should see the toy chest they have. My god, they've got two or three of *everything*. Cock pumps, biggest dildos I've ever seen, some crazy-looking butt plugs, every kind of nipple clamp known to man. It looked like a hardware store up in there. Nuts, just nuts. And lubes and lotions and creams. I tell ya, baby, it was like Christmas." He's getting all excited just talking about it all. "They've got a fucking playroom with a sex swing. A sex swing! It was wild, just wild!"

I try to pull my eyebrows down from my hairline. "So you had a good time?"

"Well, hell yeah! It was incredible. And she's a damn good fuck." I guess he sees the look of alarm on my face because he adds, "But not as good as you."

"You don't have to lie on my behalf. If she's better, she's better." I toy with the hem of my t-shirt.

"No. She wasn't better, Savannah, I promise." He kisses me. "I love you, baby."

I kiss him back. "I love you too. Want some of me before lunch?" I glance down at my crotch.

"You've always got what I'm looking for." He pushes me back down on the sofa and our brunch begins.

CHAPTER SIX

Gloria

Maybe I hadn't been paying enough attention. I got up early just to watch and, sure enough, there was a man leaving the McIntosh's house. Then a little while later, Mr. McIntosh came in. I have no idea what that's about.

I tell Russell what I've seen. "So what do you make of it, dear?"

Russell shakes his head. "I think it's none of our business, so leave them alone."

"I'm not bothering them!" He's obviously not paying attention. "I just think it's very, very strange. I don't think the neighbors would like it – at all."

"Well, we'll never know because none of them want to talk to you," he snorts.

"That's not true! We're just not close, that's all. I'm trying to remedy that, get to know some of them, you know."

"Trying to dig into their business, you mean."

Now I'm insulted. "What do you mean, Russell Livingston? I'm just trying to look out for the good of the neighborhood!"

"The neighborhood would benefit from a little less of your snooping. Leave all of the neighbors alone," he tells me as he stirs sugar into his coffee.

I'm not bothering them. But I do want to know what's going on over at the McIntoshs'. If I could just catch them together sometime – now *that* would be interesting!

I see her and I dart out the door. She's always running in and out, but I'm going to catch her. "Mrs. McIntosh! Mrs. McIntosh!" When she turns and sees me, if I didn't know better, I'd think she didn't really want to talk to me. When I finally make it to her, she looks kind of scared. I look around to see if there's a snake or a rapist or something somewhere, but I don't see anything. She's staring at me like I've got something stuck to my forehead when I say, "Hey, Mrs. McIntosh! How are you?"

"I'm well, thank you. Can I help you with something, Mrs. Livingston?"

"That's Gloria, dear." I wait, but she doesn't tell me to call her by her first name. "I just hadn't ever really gotten a chance to talk to you and I wanted to say hello. Your home is beautiful. I remember when it was built."

She smiles at me then. "Oh, really? Yes, we love it. It's very comfortable." She looks like she's relaxing a little bit from whatever was bothering her.

"That's good, dear. Say, thought any more about letting us come to one of those card games?" Card games my . . . patooty.

"I'm sorry! I forgot to ask everyone else. I'll try to remember next time." As she's talking to me, she's looking at the house. Does she think someone's in there? I thought they both were gone to work all day. If I didn't know better, I'd think she was trying to get away from me.

I have to ask – "Is something wrong, dear?"

"Uh, no. I'm just thinking about how I need to start dinner. Could we talk another time?" She's already edging toward the house. She *is* trying to get rid of me!

"Oh, sure! I'll just watch for you and try to catch you again. Good talking to you!" She turns and almost runs. That means she's hiding something. I try to keep from smiling all over my face until I can get inside, but it's hard. By the time I get to the door, I know I have a goofy grin on my face.

"Russell! Russell, where are you?" I don't hear anything. "Russell?" The bathroom door is closed, "Russell, are you in there?"

I hear him grumble. It sounded like he said, "Can't a guy crap in peace?" Then the toilet flushes. When the door pops open, he growls at me, "Gloria, what the hell do you want?"

That really hurts my feelings. "I just wanted to talk to you. I caught Mrs. McIntosh outside today."

"Oh, god, Gloria, what did you do?"

"I didn't do anything!" Why would he ask me that? "I just talked to her, asked her about the card game and if we could come. And guess what?"

He looks at me like I'm crazy. "She *did not* say we could come. I can't believe that."

"No, no, she didn't. But she was trying to get away from me as fast as she could. They're hiding something, I just know it!" I'm sure of it now, dead sure.

"Gloria, I'm warning you. Leave them alone, hear me?"

Now I'm just getting plain old mad. "I'm not bothering them. I just want to know what they're hiding, that's all."

"Yeah, yeah." He waves me off like I don't matter. "Just remember – I told you to leave them alone."

I decided I'll start dinner just like Mrs. McIntosh. The clock says it's five oh seven. That means I can take a little trip to Margaritaville while I'm cooking.

CHAPTER SEVEN

Savannah

"Would you please set the alarm clock for me?"

I lean toward the night stand. "What time, babe?"

"Three o'clock."

I look at him like he's lost his mind. "Three o'clock in the morning?"

He grins. "Yeah. Rowan and Hayden are coming over to help me."

"Help you what?"

"Install a wildlife camera." I start to understand what he's thinking. "We're going to see if we can catch her this Friday night."

"So where are you going to mount it?"

He shrugs. "Where do you think she's snooping?"

"Um, I'm pretty sure it would be a living room or dining room window. She thinks we're playing cards. Unless she's waiting until we all split off. Then I would guess a bedroom window, and there's only one bedroom on the first floor." I think for a minute. "She said she remembers when this house was built, so she may very well know the floor plan."

"That's good to know." He stops for a minute. "So what about that big tree at the corner of the lot? We can put it up high and point it at the corner of the house. It'll catch anyone at the front or side. If we see movement on the other side, we can just move it."

"Sounds like a plan!" I grin. "But what are we going to do if we catch her?"

He grins back and winks. "That, my dear, will be the fun part if we can figure out what to do."

Rowan and Hayden came over at three that morning and mounted the camera. We went out to get ice cream that evening at about ten so we could see how well it worked. It has infrared, so it worked great.

But it's the fourth Friday night of the month and time to have some fun. Everyone starts piling in. Tristan and Jasmine bring in some really yummy cheese dip. I'll have to remember to ask her about it.

We draw keys. This time I get Tate. Layla gets Tristan. Jasmine is with Hayden. Marissa draws Jeremy. Maura gets Ainsley. Makayla gets Rowan.

Angel gets Harrison. And Martin gets Stella. I'm more than happy with Tate. He's one of the younger guys in the group and he's got a lot more energy than most of the others. And somehow I've never picked Ainsley. I don't know how that's happened; everybody but him. He told me not too long ago that he was starting to get a complex. I told him if it was bothering him that much, he should tip me off the next time about which keys are his. He never has, so I guess he's just waiting for the luck of the draw. Or he doesn't want to be with me. Now *I'm* the one getting the complex.

Before we split up, Martin tells everyone what's going on with that damn neighbor woman. A couple of them look concerned; well, the women anyway; the guys seem to think it's hysterical. Before he finishes, he asks them to be thinking of something we could do if we catch her. Then everyone starts going their separate ways.

Once they're all gone, Tate asks, "Got any special requests?"

"Nope." I take another sip of wine. "Whatever happens, happens, as far as I'm concerned. What about you? Got any special requests of your own?"

"Just a blow job. You're pretty damn good, as I recall."

"That's doable. And thanks – I try hard." I give him a smile. Tate is ridiculously good-looking, almost pretty. He's barely thirty, rock-hard abs, sexy smile, and incredibly straight, white teeth. It took me awhile to figure out that he and Ainsley were college buddies. It *didn't* take any of us long to figure out that they'd been swapping out their two girls for years. Makayla and Marissa hadn't seemed to be too crazy about each other when they all began to join us, and we found out why: The guys had never let the two of them meet. They went to a hotel, one earlier and one later, with the guys switching rooms later. Then, when it was time to go, one would leave and call the other to report their departure, and the second couple would leave. The first night that Ainsley and Marissa joined us was the first time Marissa and Makayla had seen each other. It was kind of creepy the way they did that, and when we asked them about it, they said they didn't want each being jealous of the other.

Whatever works, I suppose.

We shoot the breeze for a little while. He talks about work. I talk about work. He asks where we're going on vacation this year. I ask if Makayla's about finished with school – she went back to get a nursing degree. After about fifteen minutes, he says, "Well, ready to get to it?"

"Sure!" I take his hand and lead him up the stairs. Once we're in the bedroom, he pulls my tee off over my head, then unbuttons and unzips my jeans and tugs them down. I'm in nothing but my bra and panties.

"God, I wish you'd give Makayla some pointers."

"On what?"

"Underwear." He shakes his head as I hold my arms out and pivot in front of him, my ivory and black lace bra and matching panties on full display. "You always look beautiful. She's wearing cotton panties that look like hand-me-downs from her mom and bras that are beyond worn out. It's so depressing, especially since she's so beautiful. If she'd just try a little bit, just a *little* bit. It's not like we don't have money for nice things." Tate's an attorney, so he's not kidding.

"Have you said anything to her about it?"

He shakes his head. "I'm afraid she'll get mad or be hurt, and I don't want that."

I grin. "Then take her shopping. Tell her, 'I want you to buy whatever you want. You're a beautiful woman. You should have beautiful things.' Really, Tate, you're a smart guy – why should I have to tell you this stuff?"

He shrugs. "Because I don't think like women do, I guess." He stops. "Enough about my wife. I'm here to fuck you." While he's talking, he's pulling off everything until he's naked in front of me, and he's one fine specimen. He takes his cock in his hand. "On your knees in the floor, or up on the bed?"

"Whatever you'd prefer." Some men really like to see a woman on her knees.

"Knees then. And take it deep. I like that." He waits while I position myself on the floor and reach forward for his cock. It's not especially big, but he knows how to use it. I let him have his way, threading his hands into my hair and pulling me down over his hardness over and over while I hold my hands clasped behind me. He pulls me back far enough that I have to turn loose of his dick, and then he says "Stop!" as I reach for it with my mouth. "Stay right there." He leaves and I hear him rummaging around in the closet. "Anything in here you wouldn't want me to see?" he asks.

"Nope."

"Good." In less than a minute he comes back and he's behind me. "Keep your hands behind you." Before I can protest, he ties my hands together. "Perfect! Now, let's start again."

He returns to his place in front of me and winds his fingers through my tresses again. He's just using me like a receptacle; there's no action needed on my part. Twice I gag, but it's because I wasn't ready for the next stroke. It doesn't take long for me to get into the rhythm. I feel him harden just slightly before he says, "Get ready, Savannah." Four more strokes and my mouth is full of his cum. I'd noticed before – his is thinner than most, the taste weaker. I don't know why that is, but it makes swallowing a lot easier. Once he's all finished up, he unties my hands and helps me up, unhooks my bra and lets it drop down my arms and to the floor, then pulls my panties down until I can step out of them.

"Can you find a scarf?" I'm kind of surprised. "Or a bandana?"

"Sure." I pull a bandana out of Martin's drawer and hand it to him. "What are we doing?"

"Too many questions. Turn with your back to me." Tate's pretty tall, so tying the bandana over my eyes is no trouble at all. Once he's done that, he ties my hands back together. If I'd known what he was doing, I would've let him use our cuffs and blindfold. But this is kind of exciting, not knowing what he's up to.

He takes me by my upper arm and starts to lead me, and I can tell we're leaving the bedroom. "Tate?"

"Yeah?"

"We can't go into the front of the house."

"And why not?"

"Because of the neighbor, remember?"

"Fuck her. Guess she'll get a show, huh?"

I hope Martin isn't pissed. He doesn't want to antagonize her, but it is *our* house, after all. He's very careful as he leads me down the stairs. I'm wondering where we're going, but he's already told me that

I ask too many questions. When we get to what I think has to be the kitchen, he stops. "Stand right there." I hear a door open – the garage? – and then he's back. He leads me across another room, and then says, "Here we go." He turns me around and then lifts me with his hands around my waist.

My butt plops down on something – the dining room table. I'm trying to figure out what he's doing, but I can't. He works on something behind me and then says, "Okay, Savannah, lie back." With a hand under my head, he helps me lie back without banging my skull on the table. Once I'm down, I can feel something under me, and he pulls on it. I think it's a rope attached to whatever he used to tie my hands. He scoots me forward until the tip of my tailbone is at the edge of the table, and then I feel him doing something that pulls at the rope. I've figured out that he just ran the rope through my binding and now he's doing something at each leg of the table in front of me.

As soon as he's finished, he takes my left ankle in his hands and pulls my leg up with my foot pressed against what must be his stomach. I feel something around my ankle and realize it's more rope. "Leg up!" he barks, so I lift my leg up. "Higher!" I manage to get it up so that it's straight out, and I can hear him at the end of the table at my head. I feel a tug and my leg rises higher, so high that I draw my other knee up to my chest. He's tying my leg that way, and then comes to my right side and begins to work my right ankle.

When he's done, I finally understand. The rope passed through the bindings on my wrist is tied on both sides of the end I'm facing, keeping me from sliding upward. My legs are up so high that my pelvis is flexed forward, and the bindings not only keep me from putting my legs down, but they also keep me from pulling them together too, plus they keep me from sliding downward. I'm stuck between heaven and hell and wondering exactly what he's doing.

I'm at Tate's mercy, and I wonder if Gloria is seeing all of this. Once he's done, I hear the refrigerator door open and close, then it gets really, really quiet. A chair is being dragged across the floor, and his voice moans out, "Oh, yeah. Dessert. You look scrumptious."

I almost shriek as the cold stuff hits me, and I realize he's just squirted out whipped cream all over my crotch. Someone brought it with whatever food they brought, and he must've remembered it. His breath tickles the inside of my thighs as he leans forward and starts to eat the whipped cream off my body. When most of it is gone, there's a chuckle. "Get ready, baby." I'm not sure what I'm supposed to do to get ready when his tongue starts a slow, agonizing journey up through my slit to find my clit.

I let out a moan and strain against the ropes, but they hold tight. He gets right down to business, sucking and tugging and licking until I'm squirming. Then he settles into dragging the tip of the torturous appendage around and around my swollen, needy bud, and I really start to wiggle. After just a few minutes, his finger replaces his tongue, and he puts one hand up onto my belly. "You might want to beg. I can't say it will help your situation, but it might. Up to you."

He leans up far enough to pinch one of my nipples, then the other, and I groan. Apparently he likes that, because he stands and, continuing to stroke me, he pinches and pulls first one nipple and then the other. I want to shriek but I don't, just try to take it as best I can. "Like that? Feel good?"

"Yes. Oh god, yes."

"Good girl." He keeps up the teasing with his fingertip and slides a couple of fingers of the other hand into my pussy.

"Oh, damn, Tate! Damn, damn, damn." He pumps a little, then starts to stroke my G-spot with gusto and I cry out, "Oh god, Tate, please?"

"Please what?"

"Please make me come?"

He laughs. "Oh, no. I'm nowhere near through with you yet." He keeps up the stroking, then he sits back down and his tongue replaces his finger, his strong hands gripping the backs of my thighs, forcing my legs ever farther toward my head.

Every muscle in my body is tensed and ready to explode. I'm getting close, very close. I make the mistake of groaning out, "Oh, god, Tate, I'm gonna come."

And he stops, then starts pumping two fingers into my wetness again. "Oh, please, Tate, make me come?" The pumping is fast and furious, his fingers raking the ridges on the swollen gland, and I'm so uncomfortable I can barely stand it. "Please, Tate?"

"Nope." And he stops.

I start to whine. It's all so intense that I'm almost in pain. "Oh, god!" I manage to cry out between panting breaths.

He moves to stand beside me and begins to pull and twist my nipples, then suck the one nearest him while he keeps up the torture on the other. In a few minutes, he swaps sides and does the same thing. Then I feel him move back to the end of the table. The dragging sound of the chair happens again, and I feel his tongue explore my pussy, running as deep as possible inside it followed by a vigorous lapping around my super-sensitized nub again.

"Oh, god, Tate, please?" I shriek. "Please, make me come? I need it so bad, babe. Please?" And I feel his head shake in a negative fashion.

Everything is building again, and it's more powerful and excruciating than before. "Oh, god, sweet mother of god, oh, oh, please, oh god," I keep moaning and crying. With my legs tied the way they are, I can't thrust my hips. The muscles in my belly are knotted and sore, and all I really want is that release that he keeps denying me. I want to shriek, to jerk, to pull away, but I can't. He's got me right where he wants me, and I'm not going anywhere until he's finished with his fun.

His voice is husky when he growls out, "Beg me, Savannah. Beg me for release. Tell me what you need."

I'm whining now. "I need to come! Please, Tate, let me come, please?"

"That's pretty good begging. Make it believable and I might let you." I can hear the smirk in his voice.

All I can manage is a low moan. "Oh, god, please, Tate. Oh, gawwwwwddddd . . ." My voice trails off in a moan, and I think I hear him chuckle.

"And what do you want after I let you come?"

"I want you to do whatever you want with me. Please? Just let me come." I'm desperate now and really, really afraid he's going to stop again.

He lets out a laugh. "I think you've earned your pleasure. Get ready, Savannah. I'm going to let you cut loose." The stroking is ramped up, and the next thing I know, I explode.

And I scream. I can't help it. My hips can't thrust, my legs are stiff, and I'm going crazy with the agony of it all. He keeps going until I can't think and almost can't breathe. Then he stops and leaves me panting. I feel him doing something with the rope, and quick as a wink, my legs are free and down, then my arms. And I wonder what's next.

He sits on the chair in front of me and pulls me down onto his lap – right onto his waiting cock. It's hard as steel and I cry out a little as I slide down over it, the bulbous head smacking into the end of my channel and rocking everything inside me, reminding me that his possession of my body is complete. Five strokes and I'm shaking with another orgasm, this one deep and powerful, and his smile warms everything inside me. He's really, really enjoying this, and something about pleasing him makes me smile all over. He lifts and drops me with strong hands around my ribcage, making my orgasm go on and on while he holds back, prolonging his satisfaction, offering me yet another orgasm as he waits it out. After twenty minutes and three orgasms on my part, I can feel him tense. "Savannah, this is it for me. I want you to come again with me, okay? You ready?"

I shake my head. "Almost. Can you wait?"

There's a low chuckle that escapes his throat. "Yeah. I can always wait. My control is excellent. Let me know when you're getting close."

I wonder how I'm supposed to do that when I can feel myself readying to come again. I groan at least once, my clit throbbing. He can't help but know now. "Oh, shit, oh, Tate. I'm, I'm, I'm, . . ."

A low moan escapes his lips. "I am too, baby. Let go for me." I can feel the muscles in my lower body take over, growing rigid as I shake and thrust, and he answers it all by shoving into me hard at least four times and then groaning out, "Oh, god, I can't . . ."

He holds me steady and pivots his pelvis, stroking into me fast and hard over and over until I feel him stiffen and he cries out, "Oh, god, Savannah, I love fucking you. Yeah, baby, yeah." Every word is a guttural grunt as he empties into the condom he's wearing and then drags me down onto his shaft for the last time and holds me still, his length buried deep inside me, and I'm overpowered by the sensation of warmth and power.

I collapse against his chest. Tate wears something light and contemporary, a fresh, crisp cologne that makes me think of high-end department stores and yachts and evenings in fancy French restaurants surrounded by fresh flowers and candlelight. He strokes my hair and down my back and draws in a deep, ragged breath as he tries to recover his strength. "Was I good?" I have to ask.

He pulls my face up to his and drops a soft little kiss on my mouth, then leans back and smiles at me. "Good? Yeah, you were good. You were good times ten. This is, what, our fourth time together?"

"Something like that," I whisper with a grin and kiss him back. "You know, what you lack in experience you make up for in stamina." I grin even bigger when he throws his head back and laughs, a deep, rolling sound that makes my belly quiver.

"Is that so? Well, maybe I can show you how much experience I have!" He helps me up and off of him, and I watch as he rolls the condom off his already-hardening cock. I can't believe he's going to be ready again in just a couple of minutes, but it's clear that's the case. "Come with me." He takes me by the hand and leads me back up the stairs.

"Where are we going?"

"I'm taking you upstairs to put the old guys to shame." There's a look on his face that's pure mischief, and I love it.

Once we're in the bedroom again, he just pulls me down with him into the bed. "So, care to estimate how long I'm going to be able to fuck you before I come again?"

I shrug. "Thirty minutes."

"Okay, thirty minutes it is." I expect him to rise up above me, or put me on my elbow and knees, but instead he rolls onto his side facing me, then scoots up against me and slips his cock into me again. He wiggles until I can get my leg up and under him, then throw the other one over his hip above. With that, he starts a slow thrusting into me, nothing hard or fast, just a gentle rocking type of movement. It feels good – it feels damn good. I wrap my hands around the back of his neck and he wraps his around my ribcage. The sensation is one of complete and total connection. There's nothing unknown or unnecessary between us, just the rhythm of our bodies and the soft whir of the ceiling fan above us. I wonder for a second if Gloria was peeking through the blinds downstairs, then forget about her as my body readies for release.

Two orgasms later, I'm still waiting for Tate to come. He doesn't seem to be in the least bit of a hurry. "You know, Savannah, I always like being here with you. It's just a comfortable, easy place to be. Is it this way for you and Martin?"

I nod. "Yes. Always. I love being here with him, with you, with whoever I draw from the bowl. But especially with Martin."

He gives me a gentle smile. "You guys are really in love, aren't you?"

"Yeah, we are." I smile back. Some people might think it was weird, me thinking about my husband and fucking another guy, but for all of us, it's just how it is. "We have been for a long time."

"I hope Makayla and I can hang on that long. I kind of see us as a younger version of you and Martin."

"Really? I'm flattered!" I hope my smile really conveys how I feel about what he's said. It's so sweet.

"Yeah, we get along so well and have so much fun together. The only hiccup has been the thing with the four of us."

I nod. "You mean Ainsley and Marissa."

"Yeah." He shrugs. "She's told me that if Marissa ever draws my keys and I agree to it, there's going to be trouble."

"Why? I mean, she was with Ainsley, wasn't she?" I'm trying to figure out what's wrong, and then it hits me. "This is because you two guys hid all of this from the girls?"

He nods. "Yeah, I think so. I think if we'd done things differently, it wouldn't have been such a big deal. But we were trying to keep all of it so separate, and in the end it's really worked against us."

"But why? I've never understood. Why didn't you want the girls to meet?"

He shakes his head. "We had it in our heads that if we kept them apart, that if they didn't know who the other one was, it would seem more like we were having an affair and be more exciting. And it worked. Until they met." He stops for a few seconds, then says, "I really think having them meet for the first time over here in front of a bunch of other people who knew what we'd been doing was probably a very bad idea."

I give him "the look" and reply, "Oh, I'm pretty sure you're right about that. It put them both in a really awkward spot."

"I realize that now."

"Actually," I begin, "I think what you did was make them each other's competition." He starts to speak, and I put a finger to his lips. "You were keeping them secret from each other. You obviously didn't want them to meet. Why? Were you falling in love with the other girl?"

"No. She was just a fuck. I don't mean that in a slutty way. I mean, it just didn't mean anything except a good time."

"Women don't see it that way. If you're purposely keeping her away from the other woman you're sleeping with, you must be hiding something. And now her relationship with you is obviously in danger."

He stops stroking inside me and looks into my eyes. "I see what you mean. I never thought of it that way. I guess if the tables were turned, I'd feel the same way."

I nod. "Can you go back to what you were doing? Because that felt pretty damn fine."

"Oh!" He grins and starts again, his hips undulating between my legs. "Sorry. I was just thinking. But yeah, I see what you're saying. I guess we should have a talk, huh?"

"I'm thinking probably so. And I'd suggest that you and Ainsley sit down with both of them and talk about this, the four of you."

"That's gonna take some balls."

"I'd say you've got 'em." I lean in and kiss him. It's a little surprising when he returns the kiss a little deeper and harder, and pretty soon we're down each other's throats and he's started a more purposeful rocking into me. "By the way, are you ever going to come?"

A full chuckle rolls out of his throat. "Yeah, eventually! Why, you getting tired?"

I laugh outright. "Hell no!"

"Then let's get serious about this thing." His strokes become more insistent, and I'm having trouble hanging on, but I want to wait for him.

I'm moaning and almost writhing and finally I say, "Oh, god, I need to come, Tate. Please come with me?"

He laughs and nips at my neck. "You sure?"

I nibble his earlobe, then whisper in his ear, "Sure. I'm totally sure. Oh, god..." The moan comes pouring out of me as my climax takes over, and suddenly I feel him stiffen.

"Well, it has been thirty-two minutes . . ." And it's over for him too. He presses down deep into me and grinds, the head of his cock scrubbing into me and holding the pressure I can feel at the top of my channel. His throbbing takes me down. I'm glad I drew his keys tonight. He's more than good, and I'm satisfied completely.

Twenty minutes later we're lying in the bed, staring at the ceiling, my cheek lying on his chest, his hand stroking my hair. Then out of the blue he asks this question: "Savannah, what makes you want to do this? I mean, why?"

I think about how to answer that. How can I explain it? "Well, let's see. It's not because there's anything wrong with Martin, or anything wrong between us, because there's not. And it's not because I'm a nymphomaniac." He starts to laugh. "Well, I'm not!" He laughs even harder. "Oh, stop it!" I giggle and slap his belly, and he grabs my hand and hangs onto it.

"So?"

I'm still trying to figure out how to articulate it, and I don't know how. Finally, I just say, "Oh, I don't know. I guess variety? Knowing that other men find me attractive and appealing? I'm not sure. It's like each one of you being glad that I drew your keys and not recoiling in horror is validating."

"Recoiling in horror?" Now Tate's laughing right

out loud. "I can't imagine any man doing that with you. You're a good-looking woman, and you're a hellcat in the sack. No one could possibly have a problem with you."

I shake my head. "That wasn't always the case." He gives me a puzzled stare. "Martin and I had our own variety of problems a few years back, before we started doing this. We'd gotten bored with each other, bored with our lives, bored with the sex. He suggested this; I was resistant at first. But I started thinking about it and decided to try it. The first time I was petrified, but halfway in, I realized I was enjoying myself, and it looked like I was *being* enjoyed. That kinda lit a fire under me. The four of us talked it over and pretty soon we decided we'd try to add another couple to the group. And it just went from there."

"And now it's just a staple in your lives?"

I nod. "Yeah, I guess so. I mean, I can't imagine never doing this again. I'd miss all of you, and not just you guys. All of the ladies have become friends too. But there's just something . . ." I stop.

"Something what?"

"I don't know, something erotic about knowing that my husband is fucking another woman. And that makes me want to fuck another man. And it just goes on and on. Does that make sense?"

Tate nods. "Yeah. Makes perfect sense." A

thoughtful looks lights up his eyes. "Have you ever watched him fuck another woman?"

I shake my head. "No. That never occurred to me. I think part of the attraction is that I know whatever he's doing with her, it's private between the two of them and doesn't include me. Kinda keeps me on my toes relationship-wise, if you know what I mean."

"Yeah, I can see how that would work." He puts a finger under my chin and tips my head back to look into my eyes. "It turns me on to know that I'm fucking a woman whose husband is wondering what we're doing."

I laugh. "See? That's what I mean! I guess it's that unknown factor that makes it appealing. I want to know what they're doing, and I don't want to know. Do you know what I mean?"

"I do." His hand trails down between my breasts, on down my belly, and settles in the valley between my legs. "Ah, yeah. Want some more?"

"Absolutely," I purr and lick his nipple. And more is exactly what I get.

CHAPTER EIGHT

Gloria

Well, I took myself over there to the McIntosh's after I saw all of the cars leave. They had all of the blinds drawn so I couldn't see a darn thing. I know there's one bedroom on the ground floor, but it was dark so I'm pretty sure no one was in there. And there was no way to see in the dining room or living room.

They've got to be up to something. I just wish I knew what. I'm still watching the Hendersons, Reynolds, and Millicans. I'm still trying to figure out what they're all doing, but that one time, my god, that was an awful sight, just awful. What kind of people do that? Russell says I should just let it go, but I can't. I care about my neighborhood and the people in it. If there are bad things going on, someone should take care of them. At least I think so.

I'm trying to decide what to do next. Maybe I should try again next week. I'm sure they'll have another one of those parties. And when they do, I'll be watching.

CHAPTER NINE

Savannah

"Yeah. Yeah. Uh-huh. Oh, yeah, that's good. Yeah, I'll tell her. Let's talk about it on Friday night, see what everybody else says. We'll get a better idea what's going on with her too. Okay. Okay, talk to you then. Bye." Martin punches END on his phone and turns to me with a grin.

"What was that all about?" I'm cutting up some celery for tuna casserole and he just walked in from work.

"That was Harrison. He's got an idea and I think it's pretty good. Just wait – you'll see." He's chuckling to himself as he walks away. I can't wait to hear this.

I made cupcakes, and I think they're probably the most popular thing I've ever had here for everyone because they can take a couple of them back to the houses with them. We all sit down and start snacking on the pretzels and confetti dip that Marissa made. That stuff is like crack.

Martin says, "So, we've been watching and that Livingston woman is coming over here to snoop."

"Has she seen anything?" Ainsley looks pretty concerned.

"Nah. The blinds have been drawn and the downstairs bedroom's been converted into our home office. She'd have to climb a tree to see in the upstairs windows, although I wouldn't put it past that snoopy bitch." Martin chuckles a little and everyone seems to relax. "So Harrison had a good idea."

"Yeah, okay, so here's what I was thinking." Harrison outlines the whole thing and we all start to laugh.

"Oh my god, that would be fucking hilarious if it works!" Tristan says, laughing so hard he's choking.

Maura's practically rolling. "Can we get pictures of this?"

"Oh that we could," Jeremy snickers. "I'd love to see those."

"So we look at the camera after tonight and see if she'll do what we'll bait her to do. Then we'll set everything up before next week and be ready. Baby, you know what to do, right?" Martin says, turning to me.

"Yep. I sure do." I'm still giggling. I can't wait to see this plan in action.

After everyone leaves, taking their cupcakes, of course, I do what I'm supposed to: I lever the blinds on the front door open and head up the stairs for the evening. And this time it's with Ainsley!

"I really didn't think this was ever going to happen," he tells me with a grin. "I'd just about decided that we were going to wind up in a brother-and-sister kind of relationship."

"Yeah, it was looking that way." I start up the steps, then say, "Okay, you go on up. I'll get us a couple of bottles of water apiece and some snacks. Once we go upstairs, we can't come back down, so we need to get everything right now."

I get a dish and spoon out some more of that crack dip, grab a bag of pretzels, and find two big Honeycrisp apples. Then I grab four bottles of water and put them in a bag and carry all of it upstairs. Halfway up, I run back and snatch the roll of paper towel off the holder and throw it in the bag.

"Oh, this shit is delicious." Ainsley manages to get four pretzels loaded with dip into his mouth – at once.

"Yeah, it's positively addictive." I finish off the one I'm eating. "Wait! What was that noise?"

"I didn't hear anything." Ainsley cocks his head

and listens.

I jump a little. "There it is again!"

"Okay, I heard it that time. Want me to go check it out?"

I shake my head. "No. I think we both know what that was."

He grins. "I think you're right. We'd better not go back downstairs, at least not until morning." He sneaks another pretzel and drags it through the dip before shoving it in his mouth.

"So, what do you want to do?"

He smiles at me. "Well, first, you'll think this is weird, but I want to brush your hair."

I'm shocked. "No, I don't think it's weird. I think it's wonderful." I retrieve my hairbrush from the bathroom, then sit down on the bed yoga-style and wait. Ainsley's fairly tall, so he can sit behind me and brush it, no problem. He starts a methodical stroking. "Oh, god, that feels so good." I'm groaning with pleasure.

His voice is quiet and gentle when he says, "Too many men don't do the things that their partners really need them to do. I like to take care of my women. A woman feels special if her partner takes the time to make her feel cherished."

"I like the way you think." By the time I can get the words out, the hairbrush is dropped on the floor and he's kissing me. In under five minutes, he's buried inside me and it's incredible. We spend the entire time he's here just plain old making love. Ainsley is talented, but he's also tender in a way that's erotic as hell and makes me feel passionate and adored. Martin's good, but he could take some lessons from this young man; matter of fact, I think every other man in the group could. Marissa is a lucky young woman.

We spend a little time lying across the bed on our backs, my head on his shoulder and his arm under me, staring at the ceiling. "You know, Savannah, I thought when we started this that I'd feel all freaked out that we were sleeping with other people, but now it just seems natural. Do you think the human animal was ever meant to be monogamous?"

"Nope." I drag my fingertip up his side from the top of his hip to his ribcage and he shudders. "I don't think we were. I think variety was a way to ensure survival of the species, and I also think it's only natural to have sexual feelings for more than one person. Society is the animal that's limited it, not Mother Nature. And man's desire to dominate and own one specific mate reinforced that. But I think it's a shame to limit ourselves that way."

From the corner of my eye I see him smile a lazy smile. "This is a very safe way to explore those feelings, and I'm really glad we found you guys. We're a lot younger than some of you, and yet you've made us feel so welcome and comfortable. Thanks – thanks for that. It means a lot."

"You two mean a lot. Things wouldn't be the same without you." I shift so I'm lying on my stomach, my arms folded on his chest so I can look into his face. "And after all this time, I'm glad I finally drew your keys. I was beginning to think you didn't want to spend time with me!"

"Nothing could be farther from the truth, Savannah. You're a beautiful woman, and pretty damn talented too!" He chuckles and I can't help but laugh. "Wanna get busy again?"

"You betcha!" I wrap my arms around his neck and drag him up and over me, and he hardens delightfully against me. I'll stay up all night to feel this way, his hardness filling me until I can't form a cohesive sentence or keep my eyes from crossing.

Damn, I think I'd rather fuck a hard and gorgeous man than anything else in the world. Except eating those pretzels and that amazing dip. That stuff is frickin' awesome.

We watch the video the next morning after Martin gets home and there she is. We can clearly see Gloria on the porch, and sure enough, it's about the same time I heard the noise – I'd looked at the clock and made a mental note of the time.

"So now what?"

Martin grins. "We're going to have a big surprise for her next week. I can barely wait to set this in motion. And the best part? The whole damn neighborhood is going to know something's going on. If we're lucky, at least a few of them will make it to their doors to look out and see what's going on before she manages to hide. Oh, this is gonna be delicious, baby."

CHAPTER TEN

Gloria

I sneaked over there to the McIntosh's on Friday night. They'd left the shades open on their front door. There was a light on, but when I managed to get a peek inside, I couldn't see anyone. I *thought* I did, but then there was no movement, so I'm not sure.

When I told Russell I couldn't see anything, he said, "Gloria, it's a good thing they didn't catch you or they would've charged you with trespassing."

"They can't," I told him. "It's a front porch. There's an expectation that people will walk up on it unless you've got it posted for no trespassing. No one would convict me."

"Oh, brushed up on the legalities of spying on the neighbors, huh? Sounds about right. Look, if you get in trouble poking around, I'm not getting you out of it. You'll answer to the court system, you hear me? Maybe they'll send you to rehab. That would be good, since you won't go on your own."

"Rehab?" I shrieked. "I don't need rehab! Why in the world would I need rehab?"

"Gloria, please," he said. "Stop acting like nothing's wrong."

Wrong? I'll tell you what's wrong. I'm trying to take care of our neighborhood and I'm not getting any cooperation from anyone – none. You'd think they'd be interested in what's going on right under their noses, but no one seems to be. It's ridiculous. People are doing weird, nasty things right here next door or down the street from them and they don't seem to care.

I'm going to find out what's going on if it kills me. And it might too. People like that are dangerous and devious. No telling what they'll do to me if they catch me looking for the truth.

I watch out the window this evening and I see her, so I run outside. And it's odd; unlike before, she seems to be waiting for me, almost like she's hoping I'll come over. When I make it to her, she smiles. "Hi, Gloria! What's new with you?"

Wow. That's a change of heart. Wonder if they're burying people in their crawlspace and she wants to fake me out? "Oh, nothing really. Was just wondering about that card game. Any idea if we're going to be invited to be part of the 'in' crowd?"

"Oh, I keep forgetting! Hope I remember tomorrow night. Say, would you like to come in for a drink?"

I can't believe it. She's inviting me in? Now I'm *sure* they're some kind of axe murderers, but a margarita does sound delicious right about now. "Um, yeah, sure. Is your husband home?"

"Why? Got a crush on him or something?" She's chuckling. How obscene.

"No! I was just wondering if this was 'girls' time' or something." Is she a lesbian? Is that what they're hiding? That wouldn't make sense.

"Nah, just a friendly drink. Come on in." She heads for the house with me trailing behind. I look back at my house – will Russell know where I am if anything happens to me? Hell, will he even care? We mount the steps and next thing I know, I'm sitting on the couch.

"I've got beer, wine, homemade sangria . . ."

She could've put anything in the sangria. "I think I'll take a beer, thanks." I look around. "You've done wonders with this place! It's beautiful."

"Oh, thanks! Just a work in progress." I watch her twist the top off the beer and hand it to me. Unless she injected something into it through the metal cap, it's positively fine, and I take a big draw off the bottle. Nope – I didn't fall dead. "So what do you like to do in your spare time?"

She's actually interested in me? That's a shock.

"Well, I read a lot. I love to practice mixing drinks; I have a bartender's manual and I've learned to make quite a few different ones."

"That's interesting." She sips on her wine cooler as we talk. "I'll have to sample some of your concoctions."

"Yes!" I think I'd like to invite her over for drinks one afternoon. That could be nice, her and that good-looking husband of hers. "We'll have to have you and Mr. McIntosh over some early evening."

"Please, it's Savannah and Martin." She smiles around the top of the wine cooler bottle and I wonder what she's up to.

I'm absolutely positive it's no good.

CHAPTER ELEVEN

Savannah

I laid the groundwork. That nosy bitch now thinks we're friends.

When I notice Donna Millican's car in the driveway, I decide it might be a good time to go over and ask a favor. I make my way down the sidewalk and up their front steps. I've only seen her in passing. I knock and in just a few seconds, the door cracks open. "Yes? Can I help you?"

"Hi! Um, Donna, right? I'm Savannah McIntosh. From down the street? I don't want to take up your time, but could I ask a favor of you?"

She opens the door a little farther. "Sure, I guess. How can I help you?"

"Well, we're having trouble with a nosy neighbor..."

"Oh, you too, huh?"

"You guys?"

"Oh, god, yeah. She's a real piece of work. I

know for sure that she's been over here spying. Has she been doing that to you?"

I nod. "Yep. Every chance she gets. We have these get-togethers on Friday nights and she's determined to know what we're doing. We're pretty sure she's been looking through the windows."

"Oh, god! Yeah, if there's something I can do to help you, by all means. I'll be glad to. I'll have to check with Connor, but I'm sure it'll be okay. He's pretty upset about her too."

"Well, this is what we need." I outline the plan to her, and she nods. When I'm finished, she grins.

"Oh, that sounds perfect! Sure. And I'm sure it'll be okay with Connor too. Wait – let me get my phone and get your number."

"Better yet, give me yours and I'll call it. Then you'll have mine too." She recites her number so I punch it into my phone and hear hers ringing inside the house. "Done! Listen, thanks so much, Donna. If there's ever anything I can do to help you, please, let me know. Seriously."

"I really appreciate that. Thank you. So this is this Friday night, right?"

"Yep."

"Well, good luck. I hope it works."

"Oh, if it works, you'll know," I grin. "The whole damn neighborhood will!"

"Okay, I've got the Millicans on board, so everyone can park behind their house and walk down the alleys until they can come up the back yard. What about the technical stuff?"

"Hayden's got that covered. And it'll be a scream – literally. He'll be over in the morning at about two thirty to work on it. He says it won't take long. I can't wait."

"Me neither." I'm practically itching to get going with it.

I can't help it – I can't sleep. I'm tossing and turning until I hear the back door open; Martin gave Hayden a key. He calls out, "Hey! You guys up?"

We both come bounding down the stairs. Martin's pulling on a tee and I'm in my pajamas. Hell, I've had sex with the guy. Who cares how I'm dressed, or even *if* I'm dressed? "I've been waiting for this all week. Yeah, let's get to it." Martin goes into the dining room with him and they start looking at all the paraphernalia.

"You guys want coffee?" I call from the kitchen. I get "YES" in unison, so I start a pot. Hayden's talking when I stroll into the dining room.

"So I'll wire all of these into this one switchbox. We mount the switchbox on the porch banister rung. Then, we stretch the wire across in front of the window. Not the door – anybody could come to the door. But the window will definitely be her. I'll be the last one out the door and as I go out, I'll pull the wire across and hook it on the switch. She comes up onto the porch, goes to the window, and BAM – all hell breaks loose. Ready?"

"Aw, hell yeah!" Martin laughs and they high five each other. I go to the kitchen, get their coffee, and put just a few drops of almond flavoring in it. Everybody goes on about my coffee, and that's my secret. Just enough to add something without being able to tell what it is.

They work for about forty-five minutes until Hayden says it's all ready, and then he heads back home. We go back to bed, but I'm so wound up that I can't sleep, so we just alternate between making love and fucking until the alarm clock goes off. Then the day starts. And it's going to end like no other.

We all gather on the couch. "Here's what's about to happen." Martin lays everything out, and everyone agrees it sounds like a winning idea. We take our time, eating snacks, talking and laughing, having a few drinks. Then it's time for everyone to leave.

They make sure to leave almost as a group, then stand on the porch and talk for a few minutes.

Hayden is in the back, so no one would notice him bending down and hooking the trip wire onto the switch. He nonchalantly says, "We're good," and everyone knows that means they can leave. They drive away, then come back to the next street over, turn into the alley, and pull in the back of the Millicans' house. They straggle, one couple at a time, down to our backyard, and walk up and into the back door. I've got almost all of the shades drawn – all but the one at the window where the wire is. When everyone's back inside, we decide to do something to draw her: We all start to dance. I'm pretty sure she'll be like a moth to a flame when she sees our shapes through the shades, so we just party like tomorrow's never coming.

And then it happens. I mean, I knew it was going to happen and I *still* jump! There's the sounds of a siren and an old-fashioned car horn that goes "ahh-OOOO-gahhh!" and we can see red, yellow, and blue lights flashing all over the front of the house. Everybody starts to shriek with laughter, and we all run en masse to the front door.

I can see her running as fast as she can down the sidewalk. Better yet, lights are coming on at houses all up and down the block, and dozens of people are watching her run like a bat out of hell toward her house. When I see that she's inside, I tell the guys, "Quick! Shut it off!" Hayden runs out and trips the switch, and everything goes silent. I see Donna down the street, and she's waving and laughing. Greg Henderson is at the end of his walk, looking up and down the block, and he sees all of us on the porch and starts to laugh. The Reynolds were having some kind of get-together too, and all of them have poured out of the house and are looking up and down the street. I wave to them, and they all wave back.

"Oh my god, we DID IT!" There are high fives all around and everyone is laughing and slapping each other on the back.

This is the most awesome night ever. We start all over again, and this time I draw Hayden again. And I'm really, really glad.

We've been all over each other for about three hours when we take a little break. I decide maybe it's time to ask. "Hey, how are things going with you and Angel? Seems a little better."

He nods. "Things *are* a little better and getting better all the time. We started going to counseling and they wound up diagnosing her with bipolar disorder. They put her on medication and so far she's doing really well. It's helping to level her out some and she's not so flighty. Plus she's more focused. She's actually kinder to me." It makes me sad to hear a man have to say that about his own wife.

"Good. She should be. You're a great guy."

He shoots me a tiny little smile. "Think so?"

"I know so. I hope she does better. I really do."

His smile disappears. "I do too. I really love her. I always have. It's been hard."

"I'm sure." I sit up in the bed. "Roll over and I'll rub your back." It only takes him a second to decide that's a good idea. Thirty minutes later, he's rubbing mine.

"Know what I like about being here with you, Savannah?"

"What?"

"I like that I can be myself and you won't judge me or make me feel wrong or bad or small." He looks like he might cry.

"I would never do that. It's just not who I am. You know what I think we need to do? I think we need to get some sleep. Would you hold me until I go to sleep?"

He brightens. "I'd love to." I scoot up against him, my cheek pressed into his chest, and he wraps those big, strong arms around me. And right at that moment, I'm not sure I've ever felt safer in my life.

CHAPTER TWELVE

Gloria

That was absolutely terrifying. I don't know what the hell just happened, but it was terrifying.

I just went over to the McIntosh's to see if they wanted to come over for drinks tomorrow. That's all. And when I went to the door, that's when it happened.

Noise. All kinds of noise. And flashing lights. I fell down. I was trying to run down the steps and I fell down. And I got up and fell down again because it scared me so badly. It was horrible, just horrible. I ran as fast as I could to get away from it. I don't know what all of that was, but by the time I got home, I was sweating all over like crazy and dizzy as all get-out.

And Russell was so damn mean about it. "What's going on, Gloria?" he asked. And he was laughing. I was in distress, and he thought it was funny.

"Oh my god! I went over to see if the McIntosh's wanted to come over for drinks tomorrow and all this noise started. It scared the life out of me!"

"What was it?"

"I have no idea! It was horrible, I tell you! I had to get out of there as fast as I could. There were these flashing lights and all kinds of loud noises like car horns and sirens, and I couldn't get away fast enough. And I fell down twice. Twice." I'm still out of breath and shaking.

The phone rings and Russell goes to answer it. And here's what I hear.

"Hello? Yes! Yes it is. Well, hello. Yes, she is. She's a little shaken up . . . Oh. I see." He looks over at me like I've done something wrong. "Uh-huh. Well, I don't blame you one bit. Not one bit. Yes, well, thanks for that and I'll take care of this. It won't happen again. No, you're quite welcome and I'm sorry for all of it, I really am. Take care. Thanks." He hangs up the phone.

"Who was that?"

His lips are a straight line. "That was Martin McIntosh. Seems they've been having trouble with a 'prowler.' They set a little trap for anyone who was trying to look in one of their windows." His eyes are slits. "Gloria, did you try to look in their window?"

"Well, uh, no, I just, uh, I wanted to, I . . ."

"Damn it, Gloria! You're going to keep on until some homeowner shoots you! Do you realize how much trouble you could be in?"

"But I didn't do . . ."

"You were a peeping Tom, that's what you were. You tried to look in *somebody's window*, Gloria! That's wrong on so many different levels that I can't even begin to say. One more incident – one – and you're going to rehab. I mean it. I'll have you committed." I try to say something, but he yells, "I will! I swear! Now go upstairs. I don't want to talk to you again this evening. I'm now the laughing stock of the neighborhood because my wife's the neighborhood busybody."

I can't help it – I start to cry. "But Russell! They're doing something horrible in there, I just know it!"

"You don't 'know' a damn thing. Go on. I'm sick of this. You need to go think about what you've done."

I have. And I know one thing for sure. They're up to more than I ever imagined. And I'm the only one with the balls to find out.

CHAPTER THIRTEEN

Savannah

The doorbell rings just before dinner. When I open the door, it's Donna and Connor Millican. She holds up a beautiful cake plate with an even more beautiful cake on it. "Well! What's the occasion?"

"You! That was *brilliant*! Everyone in the neighborhood is talking about it!" Donna gushes.

"I can't take the credit." Martin has come to the door to see who's there, and I go about the introductions. "You can thank Martin and a friend of ours, Hayden, for that." I catch Martin's eye and he nods. "Why don't you two come in for some coffee? We can cut this beautiful cake. I'd love to sit and chat."

"Oh, that won't be necessary. But we do appreciate you and what you did. I'm in awe, really," Connor says. There's something about him that's familiar, but I can't figure out what. "I guess we should be going. We're keeping you from your dinner."

"Oh, nonsense! You're welcome to stay," Martin adds.

"Thanks, but no. We need to get back home. But thank you for the invitation and for giving us the show of a lifetime!"

I chuckle. "Glad we could be of assistance! Please, come back anytime."

Martin and I stand and watch them head back home. She walks with her hands to her sides, and he places a hand in the small of her back. And as they go, I realize what looked familiar.

The backs of their heads. It's them – the couple from the picture in the paper. "Oh my god," I whisper out.

"What?"

"Do you know who they are?"

Martin shakes his head. "Our neighbors?"

"Yeah. And the couple from the paper. You know, the BDSM lifestyle couple?"

Martin's eyes widen. "No. You don't really . . ." He watches them walk away. "By god, I think you're right." He stares at me. "We're not the only ones, Savannah. The Millicans live an alternative lifestyle too. Who would've thought?"

Not me. Definitely not me.

On Sunday morning, I go out for a little walk. It's beautiful out, and Martin's still sleeping. He had a rough night; some things going on at work bugging him, but it'll be okay. When I pass the Millicans' house, Donna comes out the door. "Hey! Savannah! Good to see you!"

"It's good to see you too! We've almost finished that cake. Oh. My. God. It's delicious. I'll bring the plate back to you tomorrow."

"Oh, no hurry – no hurry at all. Hey, heard anything from our friendly neighborhood snoop?" She grins.

"Nope. Nothing. After Martin called and talked to her husband, I haven't laid eyes on her." I hear a sound behind me and turn to find Becca Henderson walking up. "Becca! I haven't seen you in a while."

"I know! Been busy." She reaches a hand out toward Donna. "Becca Henderson. I live down at two twenty-eight. Nice to meet you."

"And nice to meet you too! I'm Donna McIntosh. My husband Connor is inside."

Becca points to Donna's neck. "Oh, I love your pendant."

Donna fingers it delicately. "Thank you. A gift from Connor for our anniversary several years back." That's the first time I've noticed it. It's a delicate thing, a gold coin-looking pendant, and there's a design molded into it, a triskelion, and the dot within the center of each enclosed portion is really a hole. As I watch, Becca holds out her arm and there, in a tattoo inside her wrist, is the identical emblem. They lock eyes and both nod. Then it hits me.

"The newspaper. Martin was right." There's a fleeting look of panic on Donna's face. "No-no-no! It's okay! I won't say anything to anybody." I look to Becca's face. "You too?" She nods. "Then I think I should tell you: Our get-togethers on Friday nights?" They both nod at me. "We're swingers."

"Are you serious?" Donna whispers out.

"As a heart attack. So you're into BDSM?"

She nods. "Yes. We live a dedicated Dominant/submissive lifestyle." She turns to Becca. "You?"

Becca shakes her head. "No. Master/slave. Have for years." She drops her head and her face turns pink. "My Master's going to be angry with me because you found out."

"Tell him the truth. Tell him it was accidental, that we just guessed."

"Yeah," Donna adds. "Tell him we're in the lifestyle too."

"Yeah, you can tell him we swing. I don't care," I add.

"Okay. Maybe that will help. I hope I'm not punished for this."

"If he wants to punish you, tell him he'll have to punish us too," I throw in.

She grins. "Don't say that. He'd love it."

"Really?" I'm laughing, and Donna starts laughing too.

"Am I too late for the party?" Another woman strides up.

"Karen! Everybody, this is Karen Reynolds," Becca says. She points to each of us in turn. "Savannah McIntosh and Donna Millican."

"Hi, Donna! I've seen you in and out. Hey, Savannah, I saw all the commotion over here last night. What the hell?"

I do the best I can to explain and she starts laughing. "Oh my god! Wait 'til I tell Brett! He's going to get a hoot out of this! Nosy bitch has been poking around our place for awhile."

"So is she determined something kinky's going on at your house?" Becca asks.

Karen nods. "Yep. I'm afraid if she keeps poking around she'll find out she's right." She catches sight of Donna's pendant. "Oooooo, lifestyle? That's beautiful!" Her eyes fly open. "Wait! The newspaper!"

"Oh, god. I never thought anyone could recognize us," Donna groans.

"Oh, it's okay. I'm cool with it." Becca holds up her wrist so Karen can see her tattoo. "You too?" Becca nods. "Wow. And I thought we were the only ones doing something kinky around here."

"You're not. We're swingers," I offer.

"No shit! Then I guess I should tell you all: The parties we have every Friday night?" The other three of us all nod. "There are fourteen of us. We have group sex."

"You mean an orgy?" Becca squeaks out.

"Yup. Big damn orgy. We're all happily married, but it's like one huge, open relationship. Three of our girls are pregnant and, quite frankly, we don't know who fathered whose and don't care either. They'll be our babies. We'll all love them and raise them. One big happy family." She laughs and slaps my shoulder. "So what is this, 'The Kink Club?'"

"Looks like it! You know, solidarity could really help us. Whaddya say? Stay in touch?"

"Absolutely." Becca is smiling. "I think My Master will be happy to know we're not the only ones in the neighborhood that she's targeted."

"Nope. And I'm guessing she's spying on others too," Karen adds.

"I'm relatively certain of it." I laugh. "Unless maybe she learned her lesson."

Donna smirks. "Oh, yeah. Right. What are the chances of that?"

CHAPTER FOURTEEN

Gloria

It's been three days and I think my heart's *finally* stopped racing. I still don't know what to think, and Russell's still mad at me. I really don't understand why. Everything I've done, I've done for the good of the neighborhood and us. Everything.

I guess from now on I'll have to be more careful. I should probably go to the library and see if I can find a book about being a private detective or spy or something. I wish I knew how to work one of those electronic reader things, but I don't know if I could use one. If I could, I could get those books right now. But I don't mind going to the library. I've learned some very important things about the neighborhood down there from the gossip, uh, information they give each other.

But I can tell you this: It's not over. Not by a long shot. If they want to keep me out that badly, they've got to be hiding something. I don't know what, but something. And now I'm even more determined to find out what it is. That's my job. And I'm going to do it if it kills me.

AUTHOR'S NOTE

This book is the fourth of the Harper's Cove series. Join the neighborhood as Gloria does her best to find out what all of the neighbors are up to. You'll meet Karen and Brett, Donna and Connor, Becca and Greg, Savannah and Martin, and more neighbors as they go about their business, all the while thinking they're the only neighbors on the cove who have a secret to keep.

As of publication, the number of future novellas is unknown, but expect six to nine of them. So keep reading and enjoy peeking into the lives of the neighbors of Harper's Cove!

ABOUT THE AUTHOR

Deanndra Hall lives in far western Kentucky with her partner of 30+ years and three crazy little dogs. She spent years writing advertising copy, marketing materials, educational texts, and business correspondence, and designing business forms and doing graphics design. After reading a very popular erotic romance book, her partner said, "You can write better than this!" She decided to try her hand at a novel. In the process, she fell in love with her funny, smart, loving, sexy characters and the things they got into, and the novel became a series.

Deanndra enjoys all kinds of music, kayaking, working out at the local gym, reading, and spending time with friends and family, as well as working in the fiber and textile arts. And chocolate's always high on her list of favorite things!

On the Web:
www.deanndrahall.com

Email:
DeanndraHall@gmail.com

Facebook:
facebook.com/deanndra.hall

Twitter:
twitter.com/DeanndraHall

Blog:
deanndrahall.blogspot.com

Substance B:
substance-b.com/DeanndraHall

Mailing address:
P.O. Box 3722, Paducah, KY 42002-3722

Here's a sneak peek from two of the author's other titles . . .

From Planning an Addition
Book 4 in the
Love Under Construction Series

José wasn't too surprised when Molly called him the next morning and asked him to join her at a nice restaurant in town for a late Sunday lunch. Peyton, on the other hand, was surprised and very, very hopeful. Sunday was one of the nights she spent with the other guy, and he saw it as a good sign that she was opting to spend that afternoon with him instead.

Peyton was all smiles as he crossed the dining room behind the hostess. Molly was breathtaking, and the look on her face was deliciously lustful as he took a seat and asked the server for a glass of pinot grigio.

He reached for her hand and smiled. "So, what's this all about?" The feel of her fingers playing along his made his heartbeat quicken. "You said it was important."

"We have to wait. I'm expecting someone else." She took a sip of her zinfandel. Then her eyes lit up as she glanced across the room.

"Hope I'm not late," a familiar voice said as the man sat down next to Peyton.

"Hey, what are you . . ." Peyton started, but the words froze on his lips as José gave him a tiny smile. His heart seized. "Wait, you're not . . . No, it can't be. He's not . . ." Peyton gasped, turning to Molly.

She nodded. "I think it's time I came clean with both of you." Peyton shook his head in disbelief, but José was still smiling. "You should know that I've been seeing you both all this time. I've been terrified you'd find out, but you need to know." She turned to Peyton. "You really didn't have a clue?"

He shook his head again, bewildered. "No. No clue. I still can't believe it." He turned to José. "Did you know? Guess? Have any idea?"

"I figured it out." He didn't see Molly's eyebrows jack into her hairline or her mouth form an O. "She never would answer me when I asked, but the look on her face told the story. When she was with me, your girlfriend was busy. When she told me she was busy, you were with your girlfriend. Then I saw your car at her house one evening. It wasn't too hard to figure out." José still had that hint of a smile on his lips, and Peyton was starting to get a little hot under the collar.

"So exactly what do you want us to do with this information?" he hissed at Molly.

"Work it out."

"How exactly? Draw straws? Flip a coin?" Now he was just getting pissed. His girlfriend and his best friend? What the hell?

"No." Her face went sheepish. "I can't decide. I love you both. I don't want to give either of you up. I want us to be a threesome."

"Perfect!" José was over the moon. This was working out a lot better than he'd ever dreamed. And Peyton shot it all right out of orbit.

"No. Absolutely not. I can't do that." Pale and shaken, Peyton started to get up from the table, but Molly took his arm and pulled him back down into his seat.

"I think you and José need to talk this out. You know how I feel. The two of you are good friends. You need to talk about our options." She rose and pulled her sweater on as Peyton stared at her in utter disbelief. "I'm going home. I want the two of you to talk about this until you reach some kind of decision. I'll abide by whatever you work out. But know this." She leaned down and kissed Peyton, a soft, warm kiss that made his mouth water. "I love you, Peyton Stokes. You're one half of the best thing that's ever happened to me. And this guy here?" she said, pointing at José. "He's the other half. I don't want to lose you, either of you. Work it out. I mean it. I'll talk to you later." She leaned over to José and kissed him before she walked away, both men watching her ass, the sweep of her skirt melting their hearts into a puddle as she disappeared out the door.

Peyton's eyes flashed as he turned to José. "Aren't you the least bit angry about this?"

"Nope." José took a swallow of the beer their server had brought and set it back down. "Not at all. Matter of fact, I'm pretty happy."

"Pretty happy? Are you crazy? We're expected to sit here and decide which one of us gets her, like she's the last cookie on the plate or the last bite of pie?"

José leaned in toward Peyton. "Did you not hear the lady? She wants us both. *Dos. Deaux. Due.* Together. Break that cookie and keep one half. I'll take the other half. Problem solved."

Peyton ran his hands through his hair in desperation. "No. I've told you before, you people are fucked up. I'm not going there."

José's face fell. "Then there's something I think I should tell you before you go off half-cocked and totally lose it, and before I lose my nerve."

"Oh, and what's that?" Peyton snarled. "That she's really my long-lost sister? Could this get any worse?"

"Worse? Maybe. Depends on your perspective." José emptied the beer bottle and sat back in his chair.

From Adventurous Me
Book 1 in the
Me, You, and Us Series

My arms are shaking from weakness and from resting on them for so long, not to mention his body weight. Once he's beside me on the bed, he grabs me and yanks me down onto him, wrapping his arms around me. "How was that, Vännan? Was that good?"

"Oh, god, Master, that was incredible." I'm still burning, but it's a good burn.

"Wait until next time. Maybe next time you can be with me and . . . with two Doms," he corrects himself. My heart sinks. Two Doms, neither one of whom is him.

"Yeah, that would be great," I say, trying to fake excitement. This is my ninth day with him and he's still just as distant as he was the very first day. Warmer, yeah, but still distant. "Can I go to the bathroom, Master?"

"Sure! Go on," he says and slaps my ass as I get up. I go to the bathroom, pee, and throw some water on my face. When I go back to the bed, he's lying there, propped up on one elbow, and he smiles as he sees me come back.

"What?" I ask.

"Do you have any idea how beautiful and sexy you are? You're poetry in motion," he says, patting the bed beside him.

"Poetry in motion, Sir? Perhaps you haven't seen me walk in heels!" I laugh. It's true; I'm a lot of things, but graceful isn't one of them. I drop down on the bed beside him and prop myself to mirror his position, putting my face just inches from his.

"I have, and you're still poetry in motion. You've learned so much, Trish. I'm so impressed with you." *Impressed enough to collar me?*, I wonder. Nope. I'm pretty sure that's the right answer to that question.

"Thank you, Master. You're a good teacher."

He acts like he's not sure what to say. Finally, he answers, "Thank you, Trish. I'm trying, really I am."

"I know, Master. It's not even noon. What are we doing for the rest of the day?"

"I need a new car. I wanted to go look at some. Want to go with me?" he asks, running a finger up and down my arm.

"Sure! That sounds like fun, Sir." Cars. I love cars. This will be great.

"Okay. I'll pick out your clothes. No panties, no bra. And stilettos." I groan. "But they make your legs look über sexy."

"Oh! Well, in that case, maybe I need a couple more pairs, Master!"

"Maybe you do." Before I can get up out of the

bed, he presses me down, pins me by my shoulders, and looks down into my face. "We'll eat while we're out and when we get back, I plan to fuck you in the back yard. What do you say to that, sub?"

"Neighbors?"

"Yeah, we can invite them if you want." He grins.

"No! I mean, won't your neighbors complain, Sir?"

"They're not home during the day. We'll be alone. Unless one of them is playing hooky, and then they could get a worse show, don't you think?" He leans down and kisses me. His lips lock with mine and I'm lost in their warmth and softness. When he rises back up, I reach up and kiss him, just a peck. One hand comes up and strokes the side of my face. "You're really something, know that?"

"Yeah, but what?" I laugh.

"A bratty sub! You'd better get in that shower, bratty sub, or I'll have to spank your ass!" I wiggle out from under him and head for the shower. As I run I hear him say, "And a fine ass it is too."

I wish I hadn't heard that. Now I only want him more.

I hope you enjoyed these excerpts. Please be sure to check out my other titles for more reading enjoyment.

Connect with Deanndra on Substance B

Substance B is a new platform for independent authors to directly connect with their readers. Please visit Deanndra's Substance B page (substance-b.com/DeanndraHall) where you can:

- Sign up for Deanndra's newsletter
- Send a message to Deanndra
- See all platforms where Deanndra's books are sold
- Request autographed eBooks from Deanndra

Visit Substance B today to learn more about your favorite independent authors.

Made in the USA
Charleston, SC
20 February 2015